MICHELLE VERNAL LOVES a happy ending. She lives with her husband and their two boys in the beautiful and resilient city of Christchurch, New Zealand. She's partial to a glass of wine, loves a cheese scone, and has recently taken up yoga—a sight to behold indeed. As well as The Guesthouse on the Green series Michelle's written seven novels—they're all written with humour and warmth and she hopes you enjoy reading them. If you enjoy Moira Lisa Smile then taking the time to say so by leaving a review would be wonderful. A book review is the best present you can give an author. If you'd like to hear about Michelle's new releases, you can subscribe to her newsletter here: www.michellevernalbooks.com

To say thank you, you'll receive an exclusive O'Mara women Character Profile!

Also by Michelle Vernal

The Cooking School on the Bay

Second-hand Jane

Staying at Eleni's

The Traveller's Daughter

Sweet Home Summer

The Promise

And...

Introducing: The Guesthouse on the Green Series

Book 1 - O'Mara's

Book 2 – Moira-Lisa Smile

Book 3 – What Goes on Tour

Book 4 – Rosi's Regrets

October 7, 2019

When We Say Goodbye

Moira Lisa Smile

By Michelle Vernal

Chapter 1

1999

For as long as Moira O'Mara could recall, people had been telling her she was pretty. This was something which at times could be convenient. For instance, those occasions when she'd been naughty and the sight of tears welling in her big hazel eyes would get her off the hook. It could also be annoying.

She'd told Mammy just the other day she was still scarred from the little old ladies at the supermarket who'd peer at her when she was little. There she'd be, trapped in the trolley, kneeling alongside the meat, veg, and bread. She'd have been plopped in there having declared her legs were far too tired to walk any further. The temptation as those witchlike women cooed over what a wee dote she was, was to open her mouth and howl. She'd wanted to send them scarpering—stranger-danger and all that, but Moira had never been a silly girl, she knew which side her bread was buttered on, even at that age. There'd be no chance of a sweet treat at the check-out counter if she were to make a scene.

Twenty-one years later, Mammy was still not sympathetic to her plight. 'You're scarred Moira? Ha-now there's a joke. I was mortified the day you asked, at the top of your lungs mind, why old ladies had whiskers like Daddy and smelt like wet socks?'

She'd forgotten about that! Mammy always said, *For some-one with a face like butter wouldn't melt, she had a gob on her like a sailor!* The memory of that conversation made her smile as she finished the last three strokes of polish on her big toenail before moving on to the next in line.

Sure, she thought, eyeing her handiwork, it was a compliment to be told she was pretty, but it was something she'd never really got. It wasn't as if it was a talent or an achievement, something she was responsible for. She was born with the face she was born with. It was not as if she'd had any say in the matter. If anybody deserved the compliment, it was Mammy and Daddy. It was their genetics that were responsible for the way her features had decided to arrange themselves on her face. So far as she knew, nobody had ever patted them on the back and said, 'Well done. You did a good job producing her.'

Her friend Andrea once said, *It's alright for you, Moira. It's easy to be blasé about being told you're pretty when you were born beautiful. Try going through life with a nose on you that makes Barbara Streisand's look small, and at least she can sing.* She'd launched into *Memories* then, making paws of her hands, as she sang the opening lines from the musical, *Cats*. It had made Moira laugh.

There was nothing wrong with Andrea's nose; it gave her a regal air, a bit like a Nefertiti bust. Moira had seen pictures of one of those in the encyclopaedia collection Mammy had been swindled into buying many moons ago by the smiling door-to-door salesman. He'd made her think her poor children would be missing out on the basics of education were she to close the door in his face. Her mammy had always been too nice for her own good; Daddy, too. It came from being in the hospitality business. As the hosts of O'Mara's Guesthouse, politeness was ingrained in them. Aisling was the same.

She dipped the brush back in the bottle before wiping the excess against the rim. Her gaze strayed over to the bookshelf, spying the neat rows of cherry-red leather spines with their gold embossed lettering. The way the internet was going those books would be relics from the past in the new millennium.

As for Andrea, well, she was right in that she couldn't sing. She sounded like the ginger tom who'd land on the roof at night, a heavy thud followed by a stealthy pitter-patter. He liked to fight with all the other cats in the neighbourhood. Her friend might not be able to hold a tune, but she did make Moira laugh. That right there was something worthy of comment—Andrea was funny. She made people laugh. It was an achievement. The thing she didn't get where Moira was concerned was, being told she was pretty didn't give her a sense of achievement or boost her self-esteem. It was her accomplishments that did that and she could count those on one hand. Her left foot done, she put the wand back in the bottle and leaned forward on the sofa to peer closely at her painted toes. They passed muster.

She had no idea where this contemplative mood had sprung from, but she'd roll with it. Her eyes flitted to the wall where the framed painting of Foxy Loxy used to hang. She fancied she could still see the outline of trapped dust it had left behind when Mammy took it down. She'd insisted on it going with her to her new apartment in Howth—what with the painting being one of the great highlights of her baby's childhood. Moira's sigh was audible in the emptiness of the apartment. It was mad how much had happened in the last two years. *Mad!*

The very idea of her mammy, living in a swish pad overlooking the harbour was mental in itself. She could picture her welcoming her golfing lady friends, or more to the point, her pals from painting class into her apartment. She'd only undertaken the art classes in the hope it would prove it was her who'd passed on the artistic gene to her youngest child. From what Moira had seen of her attempts so far, she'd concluded it wasn't. Mammy's *Howth Pier Sunset* which she'd insisted Aisling hang in the guesthouse's reception area was on a par with Noah, her five-year-old grandson's, daubs. His latest painting, a mishmash of colours and stick figures sent over from London and titled *My Family*, was currently stuck to the fridge by magnets.

Mammy, Moira imagined would point out the professionally framed Foxy Loxy and tell her new friends, *Our Moira painted that when she was ten. It won the Texaco Children's Art Competition.* She'd pause waiting for them to ooh and aah over this accomplishment before continuing. *She was an unexpected surprise was Moira, and she's still surprising me. We always said she was gifted, her daddy and I, but she didn't take her talent any further when she left the high school.*

The latter would be said with a sad lament because Mammy had once had big plans for her youngest child. When she and Daddy accompanied her to the grand prize-giving at the Gresham Hotel all those years ago, Patrick, Roisin, and Aisling dragged along in their Sunday best, she'd been puffed up like a peacock. She'd worked the room telling anybody who cared to listen that Moira had a style similar to that of Georgia O'Keeffe. Where she got the comparison between the famous Amer-

ican artist with her penchant for big flowers and Moira's painting of the little red fox who liked to visit the bins at the back of
O'Mara's was beyond her. 'So, there you go folks, my crowning
achievement. Winning a children's Art competition,' she said.
She did that when no one was home, talked to herself. She'd be
bringing home stray cats next.

Aisling, Moira knew, called her chosen subject for the prestigious children's art competition, *Mr Fox*. The guesthouse
cook, Mrs Flaherty, called him *that fecking fox*. Her conniptions when she spotted the scraps from the bins scattered about
the concreted courtyard in the morning were legendary.

'Conniption,' Moira said, as she set about beautifying her
right toes. She liked the way it sounded and it was a word that
perfectly described their roly-poly, apple-cheeked cook's behaviour after Foxy Loxy, Moira's chosen name, visited. It was at
those times, Mrs Flaherty could turn the air blue.

Moira knew the fox lived in the Iveagh Gardens behind the
brick wall at the back of the guesthouse. She'd only ever gotten
shadowy, darting glimpses of him when she peered down from
her bedroom window to the courtyard, three storeys below.
He was O'Mara's secret visitor and some nights, she'd open her
window and drop a piece of sausage, pinched from the kitchen,
down to the courtyard below to tempt him out. Mrs Flaherty
would have combusted had she known that! It was lucky for
Moira that those wide eyes of hers filling with tears had always
worked a treat on the cook.

The day she'd decided to enter the art competition she'd
visited the library and found a book on foxes. Mammy had set
her up at the dining room table, covering it with newspaper,
and Moira had set about painting her picture from a photo-

graph in the book. She'd learned a lot about foxes from that book. For instance, she knew that they were partial to hedgehogs, a fact she'd not been impressed by. She also knew they didn't live much past five years in the wild. This meant that the Foxy Loxy of her childhood was long gone. She liked to think it was his great-grandson who visited these days. Foxy Loxy Jnr.

By the time she'd turned fifteen, she'd stopped painting. She'd been too busy organising her social life and turning her parents' hair grey. She'd stopped dropping tasty treats out her bedroom window as well, too absorbed in her teenage self. The last time she'd had a tasty treat in her bedroom, Tristan Gallagher aside, was when she'd arrived home from a night on the lash clutching a kebab. She'd woken up the next morning with the half-eaten shawarma next to her. There'd been a piece of shaved lamb nestling in her hair and she'd reeked of the garlicky yogurt sauce. Not her finest moment. It was a good thing Mammy had moved out; she'd have had her bundled up and dropped on the doorstep of the Rutland Centre for rehab, had she laid eyes on her that morning.

Moira swore softly as the thought of her mammy's new abode made her slip with the polish brush. It was weird to think how much had changed in their lives in the last two years. It was like she'd been on an out of control lift with all these stops she didn't want to get off at. She picked up a cotton bud and wiped the rogue polish off the side of her middle toe. There was no room for error, she had to look perfect tomorrow night. She wanted to prove to Michael that she could move in the same circles as him.

The shade of pink she'd chosen was the perfect match for her new lipstick, purchased at the same time from Boots. They both complemented perfectly the dress she'd spent hours looking for with Andrea. It was cerise, clung to her in all the right places, and hit the right balance between sexy and elegant. The perfect dress for The Shelbourne Hotel, and the St Tropez tan she'd had applied at great expense two nights ago ensured no pasty flesh would be on display. How was she going to get through the day tomorrow? She'd be on tenterhooks, but at least she'd be busy. The phone barely stopped ringing from the minute she put her headset on and sat down behind Mason Price Lawyers' expansive reception desk.

Today she'd actually answered, 'The Shelbourne Hotel this is Moira, how can I help?' It was only when Gilly elbowed her, she'd realised what she'd said. Luckily the client on the other end was barely listening anyway as he demanded to be put through to Brendan Dockerill ASAP! Her mind had been on nothing but the party all week.

There was only one more sleep to go until the engagement party of Posh Mairead and Niall Finnegan, one of Mason Price's Senior Partner's, and as such, tonight had been set aside for a top-to-toe beauty treatment assault. She and Mairead weren't exactly friends, so it was a miracle they'd made the guest list given its limited numbers. She'd had to refrain from replying, *We'll be there with fecking bells on*, when Mairead asked if she thought they might be able to make it along to her and Niall's low key, little celebration. If the truth were to be told she'd been as stunned as Gilly that she'd received an invite. Her co-worker had gotten her nose right out of joint about it, and Moira had had to appease her with a bag of crisps from the vending machine in the staff kitchen upstairs.

For whatever reason, however, it would seem Posh Mairead had taken a shine to her and Andrea, and as such, Moira was trying to be big hearted about her impending nuptials. It took all sorts to make the world go round and perhaps Niall had a thing for girls with buck teeth. Sure he was no oil painting himself. Moira was fairly certain Posh Mairead only worked at Mason Price because 'Daddy' had insisted she get a taste of mingling with the working classes at grass roots level. Perhaps she and Andrea were the token members of that working class on the guest list. She didn't care, the party had been circled on her mental social calendar ever since she'd received her invite.

Her eyes flitted to the fridge where the neatly printed gold embossed card was held in place by a magnet. Aisling must have brought it home from Greece given it was a donkey standing on top of the word 'Crete' and she felt a familiar frisson of excitement knowing Michael would be there.

The 'do' was to be an intimate soirée of around twenty guests in the hotel's Saddleroom. Moira had seen Niall in action and there was no doubt given his robust brown-nosing, he was a social climber. He was also in the top tier at Mason Price and as such the other high-level movers and shakers in the firm, including Michael, would be there. A bigger bash for the family and those that mattered in Dublin was being held in a month's time in the hotel's Great Room.

Moira's hair was wrapped in a towel turban, a deep conditioning treatment taking care of her split ends, and a pore minimising clay mask was beginning to tighten on her face to ensure she looked perfect tomorrow night. The word reverberated through her head, perfect, perfect, perfect; nothing less would do.

'Feck.' The phone rang banishing the word from her head. It was on the kitchen bench by the kettle where she'd left it when she'd said goodbye to Andrea. They'd run through their plans for tomorrow night and Andrea had confirmed she'd booked them both in for a shampoo and blow wave during their lunch break. Moira hesitated, torn between her toes and answering the call. She'd never been able to leave a phone to ring though, because she was far too curious by nature and besides the little voice in her head would always whisper, *what if it's something important?* She hauled herself off the couch and hobbled over, toes arched upward, and snatched the phone up.

'Hello.'

'Moira, is that you?'

She rolled her eyes. Mammy always sounded surprised. There was only the choice of two people answering the fecking thing, her or Aisling. 'Yes, Mammy, it's me. What's up?'

'Does there have to be something up for a Mammy to ring wanting to speak to her daughter?'

'Usually, yes. When the Mammy's social calendar is fuller than the daughter's.' Moira glanced down relieved to see her toes had survived their short journey from sofa to kitchen.

'I'm after some advice,' Maureen O'Mara huffed down the phone.

'Oh, yes?' Moira raised an eyebrow. Now, this was one out of the box. It was usually Mammy handing out the advice. Whether it was warranted or not wanted, it never stopped her saying her piece one way or the other.

'I'm after booking a holiday.'

Moira could hear the rain lashing against the windows and accordingly felt a stab of envy at the thought of Maureen

O'Mara stretched on a sun lounger somewhere hot and foreign. She'd probably gotten a late season week in the Costa del Sol, or maybe Tenerife; her and Daddy had gone there a few times. 'Good for you. Where are you off to then?'

'Vietnam, I'm going backpacking so I am.'

Moira dropped the phone.

Chapter 2

'Vietnam!' The sound of helicopter rotors whirring and a sixties musical medley began to play in Moira's head.

'Yes, I always fancied going there.'

'Since when?' Moira's voice rose as she cast her eyes around the empty apartment. She wished Aisling was here so she could shriek, *Mammy's after booking a flight to Vietnam and says she's going backpacking. She's officially lost the plot*! Her fingers itched to hang up so she could speed dial Roisin, her eldest sister across the water in London, with this breaking news. The toll rate was low this time of night so they could have a good old chinwag about it. This was too incredulous not to be sharing.

'I think you ruptured my ear drum, Moira.'

'Sorry, but, Mammy, come on, Vietnam? That's halfway around the world. What are you wanting to go there for?'

'Adventure, Moira. I want to have an adventure, and I want to sail on a junk.'

Ten minutes later Moira hung up the phone to her mother. She resumed her position on the sofa and finished painting her toes with swift, efficient brush strokes, her brain whirring. The advice Mammy had been seeking was whether she should spend the money on having a yellow fever jab as a precaution before she went. Apparently, it cost a small fortune, but it was advisable when getting off the beaten track. 'For feck's sake, Mammy you're not after jungle trekking or the like surely?' Moira had exploded. This was all too much to take in.

It would appear that Mammy was planning just that, and she was going on some rowboat down a big river too. Moira wasn't sure if they had hippopotamus's in Vietnam or not and the thought made her shudder. Only the other day she'd caught the tail end of a wildlife programme on when hippos attack. She was fairly sure they were only found in Africa but fairly wasn't one hundred per cent. She'd already lost her daddy, she wasn't going to lose her mammy too. And alright, maybe you couldn't call a short jaunt from some tribal village in the mountains jungle trekking, but still and all it was bad enough. Mammy had informed her she and her travelling companion, Rosemary Farrell from her rambling group, had been practising by taking to the hills around Howth.

Moira had latched on to this. 'Mammy, Howth is not a tribal mountain village and adventures aren't for women in their sixties.' They certainly weren't for mammies in their sixties! 'Sure look it, why can't you and this *Rosemary*,' she'd already pegged her as a bad influence and she pronounced her name accordingly, 'have a nice walking holiday together down in Connemara or Mayo? Everybody knows there're loads of lovely trails around there you could explore. Listen, I'll even spring for one of those pole thing-a-me-bobs older people are so fond of hiking with if you change your plans.'

'Moira O'Mara, I've only just turned sixty and that was a non-event. None of us felt much like celebrating now, did we? This is my belated birthday present to myself and, for your information, young lady. I'm not a geriatric and there are no junks in Connemara or Mayo. I want to sail on a junk. I have done since I saw James Bond escape on one in *The Man with the Golden Gun*. It's on my list.'

She'd sounded like a belligerent two-year-old stamping her feet, and what was she on about? 'What list?'

'My list of things I want to do before I join your daddy.'

'Ah, Mammy, sure don't talk like that. You've years left in you. You don't need to start ticking things off a list.'

'Your daddy and I thought we had years left together. None of us know what's around the corner, Moira, and I don't intend to sit on my backside waiting for my number to be called.'

Moira chewed her lip, unsure what to say. They'd all handled Daddy's death nearly two years ago now, differently. Mammy had announced she wouldn't see her days out in the guesthouse without her husband at her side. Her ultimatum had been, either one of the O'Mara children step up to manage the business, or it would be sold. She'd then set about buying her apartment in Howth and joining the golf club, taking art classes, enrolling for sailing lessons, and putting her name down on every social committee the seaside community had to offer. In short, she'd gone completely round the twist.

It was Aisling who'd taken hold of O'Mara's reins. Her way of coping with her grief was by immersing herself wholly in the family business. Thank goodness she and Quinn had taken their blinkers off where each other was concerned; her sister had a much better work life balance going on since they'd hooked up. She'd been very bossy before, overly interested in what Moira was up to, and forever on at her to straighten her room up. Now she was all loved up, she was still annoying in a *my life is soo wonderful way*, but at least she left Moira to her own devices.

Moira didn't know how it was for Patrick and Rosie knowing Daddy wasn't in their lives anymore. Being away, they were removed from the day-to-day reminders of him. She still felt his presence in every room of the top-floor apartment of the Georgian manor house where she'd lived her whole life. Her breath caught, she missed her lovely, generous, kind father every minute of every single day. Mammy dragged her back into the conversation.

'I'll have you know just the other day Terry Lynch from the butcher's was after telling me I didn't look a day over fifty. He gave me an extra chop, too, so he did. And, Moira O'Mara, I'm the same age as yer Fonda woman and nobody'd bat an eye if she announced she were off trekking. So, as a grown woman, your Mammy no less—something you'd do well to remember my girl, don't be after telling me what I should and shouldn't do!'

She'd sounded very huffy and had hung up without saying goodbye. Moira was not in the mood to call her back. She knew from the tone she'd get the mortally offended version of Maureen O'Mara were she to do so and she'd be made to feel so guilty, she'd have to apologise. But if she apologised it would mean she approved of this trip to the wilds of Asia and she most certainly did not. No, she'd leave it for now and let Aisling or Roisin try to talk some sense into her. Mammy would not be going to Vietnam if Moira had anything to do with it.

Chapter 3

M oira breathed a sigh of relief as she heard the front door open. Aisling was home, she'd know what to do about Mammy.

'Jaysus, it's wild out there tonight,' Aisling said, rubbing her hands as she came into the living room. Spying her sister, her eyes narrowed. 'Moira get your feet off the table.'

'Aisling, feck off, there're bigger things to be worrying about than my feet on the coffee table.' She felt the face mask crack as she spoke, a reminder that she should be in the shower by now.

'Such as?'

Moira removed her feet knowing she wouldn't get her sister's full attention until she did so. She glanced beyond Aisling checking to see if Quinn was behind her. He wasn't. She loved Quinn but a night off listening to the pair of them riding like they were trying to win the Grand National was welcome.

'Mammy's only gone and got it in her head to go to Vietnam for nearly a month with some rambling woman and she's going tribal and, and, and I don't know if there're hippos there or not.'

'Jaysus, it's like a sauna in here. Have you turned the heating up?' Aisling shrugged out of her jacket. 'No wonder you're babbling like a mad woman.'

Moira had adjusted the dial on the central heating but she wasn't going to admit to it. The two sisters had a constant battle over the setting. Aisling liked it to take the edge off while Moira preferred it hot enough to close her eyes and imagine she was somewhere like Spain, not fecking Vietnam! It was a country that had never been on her radar until tonight and Aisling wasn't giving her the aghast reaction she wanted.

'You're not listening to me!'

'Moira,' Aisling held her hand up. 'Stop and breathe.' She eyed her sister and shook her head. 'I don't how you expect me to take you seriously looking like that.'

If Moira could have scowled, she would have, but the face pack wouldn't stretch to that. She did, however, slow her breathing. She needed to be coherent.

'Right, now start at the beginning, only slowly this time.'

'Okay, what it is, I've not long got off the phone to Mammy. She told me she's booked a holiday to Vietnam with a woman she goes walking around Howth with. Rosemary something or other. I don't like the sound of her. I think she's trouble. Anyway, they're planning on doing a hill trek and sailing down some river and everything. She's got it in her head she wants to sail on a junk. Do they have hippos there?'

'No, you eejit, they're only in Africa.' Aisling frowned. 'Rosemary. That name sounds familiar.' She flopped down on the end of the sofa. 'Wasn't that yer woman who had her hips replaced? I'm sure Mammy told us a story about her setting the sensors off at the airport with whatever the doctors replaced them with. Kryptonite or something. No, hang on that's Superman; titanium, that was it.'

'Ah, Jaysus, it gets worse.' Moira rubbed her temples, the image of her mammy and this Rosemary Farrell getting patted down by airport security was too much.

Aisling slid her feet from her shoes and flexed them. 'Ooh, that's better. I'm sure I'll hear all about her travel plans on Saturday afternoon.'

Moira had forgotten about that; her head had been so full of the party. They were going to have afternoon tea at the Powerscourt Hotel, Mammy's treat. She'd have to apologise if she wanted her slice of cake.

'I don't know what you're making such a fuss about, though, Moira. Mammy's a grown woman. I was reading in one of our magazine's in reception that Vietnam is establishing itself on the South East Asia tourist trail. She'll be fine so long as she doesn't decide to befriend any strange men who ask her to carry their excess baggage through.' She rubbed her soles one after the other. 'I've been on my feet all day.'

'That's not funny and being on your feet all day makes a change from on your back.'

'Moira!'

'Well, it's true! You and Quinn are like rabbits.'

'We're making up for lost time.' Aisling got the daft look on her face she always got of late when Quinn's name was mentioned.

Moira had been gobsmacked the morning she got up to find Quinn, a chef who ran his successful bistro by the same name, sitting at their breakfast table. She still wasn't over the shock truth be told. Her sister had been good friends with him since her student days. Friends being the operative word, or so she'd thought. It turned out they'd both been in love with one another for years but it had taken the threat of Aisling going back to her ex-fiancé for Quinn to act on his feelings. Personally, Moira thought it was down to the salsa classes they went to; all that hip gyrating was bound to stir something up! She blamed the saucy Latin American moves on her sister having turned into a loved-up pain in the arse overnight. Speaking of which, she thought, tuning back into Aisling.

'But for your information, we've been at salsa class tonight and I had a mad day downstairs. One of the guests, Mr Rankin, missed his tour and I had to tee him up on another as he's only here for two days, then Mrs Flaherty had—'

'Conniptions,' Moira jumped in, eager to use the word once more.

'Yes, over the Ardern family's dietary requirements. You know she doesn't believe in such things.'

Moira smiled. Mrs Flaherty's idea of dietary requirements was a good stodgy Irish fry-up cooked in lashings of lard and woe betide anyone who disagreed with her.

'Then I had to give Ita short shrift. I caught her sitting on the side of the bath in Room 3 instead of making the room up like she was supposed to be, playing some game on her Nokia.'

'Snake,' Moira said knowledgably, having recently been caught doing the very same thing by Mr Price himself, Mason Price's fusty old senior partner. 'I don't know why you put up with Idle Ita.'

'Yes, you do.'

'Alright, but Mammy's not in charge any more, she's retired. You're O'Mara's manager which means you're no longer obliged to keep her friend's daughter on. Sure if work was a bed that one would sleep on the floor.'

'I know but still—'

'You're a scaredy cat, Aisling O'Mara.'

Aisling couldn't argue, she was where Mammy was concerned. Moira was the only one who said her piece on a regular basis.

'But I still want you to talk Mammy out of this Vietnam business.'

'Moira since when has anyone ever been able to talk Mammy out of anything. Sure look it, you know how it goes, Mammy tells us what to do not the other way around. It's the way it is. I can't upset the status quo.'

Moira tried to frown but couldn't. Aisling was right. The only person she might listen to was Patrick but her brother was too caught up in his new life over in the States to care much about what was happening here. She felt the familiar sting at his absence; she missed him and wished he'd make a bit more time for them. The last few times she'd called he'd been heading out the door to some function or other with that silicon-infused girlfriend of his, too busy to ask how she was doing since Daddy died. That left, Roisin. The odds were slim of her words holding any sway but given her seniority as the oldest daughter, she should at least try. It was her duty, Moira thought knowing it was too late to call her now. It would have to wait until the morning. She realised Aisling had moved on.

'Then I had to move Mr and Mrs McPherson from Room 8 because the shower was playing up. It was lucky we had Room 4 available and, to be fair, they were very good about it. Then, I spent the best part of the afternoon trying to get hold of a plumber, and you know how hard it is to get trades people these days.'

She did, Dublin was booming and as such trying to nail down a plumber, or any tradesperson was like trying to find that pot of gold at the end of the rainbow. It was also the reason why she had to listen to the headboard banging of a night. Accommodation was at a premium and she couldn't afford to move out and maintain a social life. For the time being she was stuck at O'Mara's with its memories of her daddy lurking around each and every doorway.

'I finally found an outfit who promised to send someone out for a look before lunchtime tomorrow so that means they'll be here around five o'clock. I'd no sooner hung up the phone than Tessa Delaney, who arrived yesterday—she's in Room 1—wanted to know what the kerfuffle in the middle of the night was all about.'

'Foxy Loxy?'

'Mr Fox,' Aisling confirmed. 'No doubt I'll get it in the ear from Mrs Flaherty. She's a bit of a strange one, I can't put my finger on it.'

'Mrs Flaherty is Mrs Flaherty, a heart of gold, a mouth like a sewer, a lover of food, and hater of foxes.'

'No, not Mrs Flaherty, Tessa Delaney.'

'Is she yer one from New Zealand? I overheard her asking Mrs Flaherty if she could have her *eeeg* served over easy. I made her say it again. I liked the sound of it.'

Aisling nodded. 'Mmm, although she's from Dublin originally. You'd never know it from listening to her; she's no trace of an accent left. I only managed to find that out because I suggested the open-top bus city tour was a good way to get her bearings. Her parents emigrated when she was a teenager. This is the first time she's been back.' She pursed her lips. 'I don't know what it is about her.'

'She seemed friendly enough to me. She'll find Dublin's not the backwater she left behind.'

Aisling nodded. 'It's a different city alright.' The influx of visitors since the Celtic Tiger had started roaring had been great for the guesthouse's business and the streets hummed with the vibrancy of its many visitors. 'And she's friendly enough. I got the feeling she wasn't honest about her reasons for coming back to Dublin that was all.'

Moira shrugged. 'Maybe she's jet-lagged. She has travelled from the other side of the world and she's in a different time zone. I had enough issues going to New York with Andrea last year; my poor tummy was telling me it was dinner time when it was bedtime for days. You know what you're like, Ash, you always see more in a situation than there is.' This was true. Aisling's imagination was prone to running away with itself.

'I suppose it's because she comes across as a closed book; I want to take a peek inside. There's definitely more to her coming back than a simple trip down memory lane. Besides, she had a week in London before coming here. That's plenty of time to get over the jet lag.'

'So you know her parents left Dublin for New Zealand when she was a teenager and she's had a week sight-seeing in London? And, I just told you she likes her eggs over easy.'

'Mmm. What's your point?'

'You should have been a detective, Ash. What more do you want to know? How she likes her fecking steak? It's none of your business.'

Aisling poked her tongue out at her sister and picked up the television remote, 'The Late Late Show's on soon.'

'Ah, it's not the same without Gay Byrne.'

'He's only been gone a couple of weeks, give Pat Kenny a chance.'

'Not tonight, I've got to go and wash all this off.' Moira gestured to her face and the towel.

Aisling's gaze flitted to her sister's toes, back on the table once more. She let it slide. 'I like that colour.'

Moira pointed to the bottle of polish. 'I'll let you borrow it if you let me wear your red Valentino slingbacks with my dress tomorrow night.'

Aisling shook her head. 'Nope, no way.'

'Oh, please, pretty please. They'd be perfect.' That word again.

Aisling's eyes narrowed. 'So that's what this is all—,' she gestured to her sister's face and hair '—in aid of.'

Moira nodded. 'It's Posh Mairead's engagement party and you know how long I've been looking forward to it. Please, please, please. You're my favourite sister.'

'Liar, I heard you saying the same thing to Roisin not long ago and I still haven't forgiven you for wearing my Louboutin's without my permission.'

'You need to let it go. It's not good for you to hold on to stuff like that. I said sorry a million times. It was ages ago.'

'I'm not talking about when you got a scratch on the heel. I'm talking about when you sneaked out in them a month ago.'

Moira flushed beneath the clay. She'd thought she'd gotten away with that.

Aisling looked jubilant and Moira realised she must have stored the misdemeanour away, waiting for the right moment to use it. Feck it, she really wanted to wear the shoes.

'You could try splashing your cash on a pair of your own.'

'Sure look it, Aisling, what would be the point? Not when I've a sister whose fashion sense is second to none.'

'Flattery won't work. I want something more.' Aisling hit the mute button on the television.

Moira pouted, 'Like what?' She was envisaging having to tidy her room like Mammy had always made her do of a Saturday morning when she was younger. Or worse, having to clean the bathroom, her most hated of all household chores. Housework was not her forte. What her sister said next took her by surprise.

Chapter 4

'I want to know why the secrecy every time I ask whether you have a new fella on the go?' Aisling said.

'There's no secrecy.' Moira's voice had a high-pitched intonation which she knew would not escape her sister.

'Do you want to borrow the shoes or not?' Aisling narrowed her eyes.

Yes, she did, but Moira hesitated. She was a truthful girl. There were some who might say she was too inclined to tell the truth, the whole truth, and nothing but the truth. There were some who might even go so far as to say that a little white lie for the sake of diplomacy wouldn't go astray here and there. It wasn't her style though. She'd never been one for subtleties or for unnecessary platitudes. She was what was known as one of life's blurters. It was the Mammy gene, and no course was needed to find out if it was inherited from the maternal side of the family. Therein lay her present dilemma. She wasn't prepared to tell Aisling or anyone else—Andrea being the exception of course. given her best friend status—about Michael.

It wasn't that she wanted to protect Michael, even if he had asked her to keep whatever it was happening between them to herself for the time being. She would of course. She'd do whatever he asked her to do because she wanted to be with him in a way she'd never wanted to be with anyone else before. Her reason for being discreet was for selfish reasons. She knew she'd get an almighty lecture. Her mask would be flaking off her face and her hair dry beneath the towel by the time Aisling had finished with her if she were to reveal Michael wasn't actually hers for the taking. It would be an understatement to say her sister wouldn't be impressed if Moira were to tell her the truth. She'd go mad, and then she'd ring Mammy. It was a given that this was what would transpire if Aisling learned her new love interest was married.

'You've gotten awfully furtive of late, Moira O'Mara.'

Aisling reminded Moira of Foxy Loxy at that moment with her reddish-gold hair and narrowed green eyes. 'I haven't.' She knew she had, but needs must.

'Yes, you have. It's little things, like the way you're so sneaky with your phone, and you never tell me who you've been out and about with.'

'I wouldn't call not telling you everything I do furtive, I'd call it my business, not yours. The only reason I don't mention who've I been getting about with is because nine times out of ten it's Andrea. There's no big secret.'

Aisling was undeterred. 'Sorry, I'm not buying it. It's that smile of yours. It gives you away.'

'What smile?'

'The one you always give me whenever I ask you who you're seeing. You'd have done it when I asked before only you can't move your mouth under all that clay. It's really annoying. Actually, it's more than annoying, it drives me potty.'

'I still don't know what you're talking about?'

'This, you do this,' Aisling attempted to demonstrate.

'Jaysus, you look constipated.'

She scowled. 'I call it your Mona Lisa smile, and like I said it's doing my head in. So, either spill the beans and look a million dollars in the Valentino's or, keep your little secret, whoever he is. It's no skin off my nose if you totter about your posh party in those high street heels of yours. The ball's in your court, sister.'

Moira weighed up the odds. This was one of those rare occasions when, for the greater good, she'd have to tell a half-truth. The very thought made her squirm but her moral code was being trampled all over by her desire to wear the perfect shoes with her perfect dress. 'Alright then,' she said licking her lips. 'You win.'

The smug look on Aisling's face irritated her as she leaned in to hear what she had to say.

'You're right, I am seeing someone.'

'I knew it.'

'I didn't mention it because it's early days, very early days. I don't know why you're making a thing about it. We're only just beginning to get to know one another. We haven't even done the wild thing yet, not even close.'

'There's nothing wrong with waiting, Moira.'

'Says the woman who ripped Quinn's clothes off the moment she realised he fancied her.'

Aisling ignored her. 'Tell me about him.'

'He's from London originally. Mason Price headhunted him from a rival firm over there and brought him over a couple of months ago as partner in the Aviation and Asset Finance Department.' She saw her sister fidget in her seat and read her mind. 'There's no point in you running off downstairs to reception to see if you can find him on the website, he's not on it. He's not been with the firm long enough for them to get round to updating it.'

Aisling looked disappointed but pushed it aside to demand, 'Name?'

'Michael.'

'Michael.' She tried it out for size. 'It's a respectable name, not like Leila's new man. Did I tell you he's called Bearach which she tells me means Barry?' Aisling snorted. 'She's getting serious about him so I'm going to have to get used to pairing them together without laughing.' She gave it a practice run. 'Bearach and Leila, Leila and Bearach.' Her mouth twitched with the effort to keep a straight face.

'Ah sure, give the poor girl a break. He's probably a really nice fella and you're in no position to laugh and point fingers. You've dated your fair share of eejits, one ex-fiancé included.'

'It's true alright. I had to kiss a frog or two to find my prince.' Aisling got that daft, dreamy look on her face again. It was the look that signalled she was having indecent thoughts about Quinn, and Moira made to get up from the sofa and make her escape.

Aisling blinked, obviously banishing Quinn for the moment as she wagged her finger. 'Uh-uh, I'm not finished yet. How old is he, this Michael fella?'

Moira paused, it suddenly mattered to her very much that her sister not disapprove of Michael.

'A-ha!' She slapped her thigh. 'I knew there was something. That's why you've been such a secret squirrel where this Michael is concerned. Come on then, is he ancient?'

'He's thirty-eight for your information, hardly ancient.'

'Old enough to be your father, though.'

'Not unless he was at it when he was thirteen, Aisling.' Moira decided to play the pity card. 'Sure, there are no decent fellas around my age, Aisling. They're all feckless tossers. Michael treats me like an equal and I love his confidence, his worldliness—,'

'His ancientness, and what's with the love word? I thought you said it was early days.'

'It is and I was speaking metaphorically. Thirty-eight is not old, Ash. He's the same age as Patrick. I bet you don't think of him as being old and his girlfriend, Cindy is only a year older than me.'

Aisling shuddered, 'Our brother and his choice in women isn't a good example, Moira. I don't think he asked Cindy out because he felt they were on the same intellectual footing and therefore would be able to engage in stimulating banter. Do you?'

Moira didn't, but now wasn't the time to concede. 'I knew you'd react like this, that's why I haven't said anything.' This time she stood up. 'You all treat me like I'm a kid in this family.' Sometimes the nearly ten years between her and Aisling felt more like twenty.

'A teenager at the very least.' Aisling grinned.

Moira muttered something rude before adding, 'Anyway the Valentino's are mine for the night because I kept my side of the deal and that's all I'm saying on the subject.' She flounced toward the door, turban wobbling, and paused as she reached the hall. 'And don't you dare tell Roisin or Mammy,' she threw back over her shoulder. 'I mean it, Aisling.' Her life would not be worth living if Mammy were to catch wind of the fact her prodigal daughter was dating an older man and if she found out he was married, well she might as well hightail it to Vietnam herself because she'd never hear the end of it!

Chapter 5

M oira wiped the mask off with a flannel and eyed the grey residue before rinsing it out and holding her face towards the hot jets of water. It felt nice to be able to move her face properly once more. She stretched her mouth into an 'O' shape for good measure knowing her skin would be rosy, pink, and soft from the treatment. She closed her eyes for a beat and her mind drifted back over her conversation with her sister.

Mammy and her impending trip had been forgotten once they'd gotten onto the subject of Michael Daniels. Aisling had been aghast at his age. It was annoying given nobody in the family had batted an eye over Patrick's new plastic-fantastic being younger. This wasn't the dark ages it was 1999 for feck's sake. She was a twenty-five-year-old woman capable of forging her own path and making her own choices and way in life. I mean sure look it, here they were on the verge of a new millennium with the threat of Y2K and the like looming. The IT Department at work had been scrambling all year trying to put programming corrections in place to protect the firm's software. She'd heard talks of the bug having catastrophic effects like the banks going down; there could be widespread chaos. So, if Aisling were to look at the bigger picture, her new man being a little—alright over a decade older than her—was not a big deal in the grand scheme of things, not with the end of the world as they knew it nigh.

She never thought about Michael's age on those snatched rare moments they managed to be alone. It was irrelevant. What mattered was the way he wanted to hear what she had to say. He wasn't just listening with half an ear while thinking about how he could get into her knickers, he genuinely heard and cared about what she was saying. He made her feel special, worthwhile, in a way no one else had done before. She'd only known him a short while, and they'd only exchanged one proper kiss in that time, but oh, what a kiss. It had hinted at the promise of things to come. She'd never fallen this hard and fast for anyone, no matter what she'd said to Aisling about taking things slow.

She tried not to think about him being married and if she'd come clean with Aisling, Moira knew she would have rolled out the clichés in his defence. His marriage is in name only, he and his wife lead separate lives etc, they're only together for the sake of the children. At that point Aisling would have exploded, hand raised like an army sergeant as she shrieked, *Stop right there and back up. Did you say, children?* It would have swiftly been followed by finger pointing and the word homewrecker would have been wielded like a slap.

Moira wasn't proud of herself, or the situation she'd found herself in, far from it. She hadn't set out to fall head over heels for a married man but if that marriage was broken, irretrievably so, how could that make her a homewrecker? Surely the home was long since wrecked. She didn't know the answers and didn't want to delve too deeply in case she didn't like what she found because she was too far gone to walk away from Michael now. Her daddy's face flitted before her and she felt her eyes burn beneath her closed lids.

He wouldn't approve of what she was doing. She knew that, but then he'd always been protective of her, of all three of his girls but especially her being the baby. Mind you, he'd have struggled to approve of the future King of England when it came to his youngest daughter's choice of beaus. She grimaced, she didn't fancy Prince Charles in the slightest and had no idea where that weird comparison had come from. The fact of the matter was though, if her daddy was here now and knew what she was up to he'd be bitterly disappointed in her, and that would be worse than any histrionics or disapproval her sister could serve up. 'The thing is, Daddy,' she whispered into the steam, 'you went and died and the only person who's made me feel happy, made me feel anything at all since you left us, is Michael.' Moira tasted salt on her lip. 'Is it wrong to want to be happy?' She ignored the voice that whispered back telling her it was if it was at someone else's expense. The water continued to wash over her as she shook the maudlin thoughts away swinging her mind toward the night she first laid eyes on Michael instead.

Chapter 6

When she first saw him...

'I wish old Fusty Pants Price would buy a new suit. I'm sure he's owned that one since the year I was born,' Moira whispered out the corner of her mouth to Andrea as Mason Price's senior partner entered the boardroom. He was like the king on a Friday night walkabout to greet the commoners. It always amused her the way the partners all stood a little straighter when he appeared. The secretaries and the rest of the minions didn't bother, too focussed on making sure they got their quota of the free drinks chilling on ice that were on offer for the Friday night session.

'Mmm, the colour poo brown springs to mind and wait a minute—well, hellooo sexy, who is that?' Andrea's eyes widened over the rim of her wine glass and her hand froze over the bowl of potato crisps she'd been about to dive into as she checked out the stranger. 'There's a new boy in town.'

'I thought you only had eyes for Connor Reid.' Moira looked past Mr Price to the unfamiliar, handsome face that had materialised behind him. She didn't get much of a chance to check him out other than to note his hair was the colour of dark chocolate with streaks of silver around his temples, nothing poo brown about it in the slightest, and his eyes were blue. They made for a startling contrast against his dark hair she thought as he turned away. Fusty Pants was introducing him to

John Bryant, eejit that he was, from Finance and she watched John Bryant's hale and hearty *I'm one of the lads* handshake with disdain.

It was unusual for her not to know a face given her front desk position. She knew everyone from the catering staff and IT gang, through to the secretaries and the solicitors they worked for, by name. It was her job to. She'd greet the various staff members as they breezed importantly through reception. It hadn't taken Moira long to realise it was part of Mason Price's job description to look as though you were on important business at all times even if you were just on your way to the loo. Perhaps this handsome stranger was a client whose meeting had run over and Fusty Pants had suggested he join them for a drink? Whoever he was she determined, looking at the way his elegantly cut navy suit with its faint charcoal pinstripe hugged his derriere—snuggly but not too snuggly—she'd find out.

She smiled a *no thanks* to Ciara from catering who had appeared in front of her and Andrea with a tray of sandwiches. Andrea, however, was not going to miss out and she nearly knocked Moira's drink from her hand in her eagerness as her arm snaked out and she helped herself to two of the triangles. Egg breath was not the order of the day, Moira thought with a sanctimonious glance at her friend's stash, even though she was partial to an egg sarnie.

'I do, but Connor's not realised he's only got eyes for me yet so I am allowed to browse elsewhere.' Andrea mumbled, stuffing the sandwich in.

Moira sipped her wine, all the while keeping her eyes trained on Blue Suit as she'd already nicknamed him in her head, while listening to Andrea's tale. It was a convoluted story

about the injustice wielded upon her poor self that very afternoon by Nora McManus, the solicitor she worked for in the
Tax Department.

'Up herself, unreasonable, self-important, cow. Honestly
one of these days I'll tell her to stick her job where the sun don't
shine.' Andrea had finished with the sandwich, so she turned
and speared a meatball off the platter on the table behind them
with a cocktail stick.

Moira shot her a sideways glance; they both knew this
wasn't true. Andrea would stay right where she was. For one
thing, Nora McManus was scary and it would take a stronger
woman than Andrea to stand up to her, and for another, sometimes it was better the devil you know.

'It's not my fault she always leaves everything to the last
minute and then expects me to type two hundred words a
minute so she can file her stupid documents in time. I'm not
bionic for feck's sake,' Andrea muttered, popping the meatball
in her mouth and chomping angrily. 'I always eat when I'm
stressed. Stress is not good for my figure. I'd be as svelte as Kate
Moss if mealy-mouthed Melva would hurry up and retire. She
must be fecking ninety if she's a day; then I could be Connor's
right-hand woman.'

Moira knew she was her friend's sounding board. She needed to vent after having smiled sweetly at her boss all day as she
told her she'd do her best to get the work completed in time.
Listening to Andrea made her glad she didn't answer to one
particular partner, she didn't think she'd last very long if she
did, because she was nowhere near as diplomatic as Andrea.

'Ooh, ooh,' Andrea mumbled through her mouthful. 'He's
turning around, we're going to get a full frontal. Wait for it!'

Moira noticed they weren't the only women in the room checking out Blue Suit. A new face, especially a handsome new face in the firm, was big news. The Property girls and Ciaron were huddled together in their usual cliquey manner, all gawping while trying to pretend they were fascinated with the painting hanging on the wall behind him. It was at that moment Blue Suit looked across the room to where she was standing. Moira felt as though someone had hit the mute button on the television; there was no sound, everybody else in the room faded out as though they'd never been there in the first place. It was just the two of them. Those electric blue eyes appraised her and when he smiled a sensation that made her blush pulsed through her.

'Smile back, you eejit,' Andrea muttered, and she did as she was told.

She watched, secretly pleased to note that Mary from the Litigation Department, who wore her skirts way too tight, was simpering up at him blissfully unaware of the piece of cress stuck to her lip. Served her right, Moira thought. She'd obviously not had the willpower to decline the egg sarnie.

Fusty Pants and his mystery cohort had worked the best part of the room by the time they finally reached their corner. Moira was hopping from foot to foot with impatience, waiting for an introduction. She leaned back against the boardroom table, feigning nonchalance. The realisation that there was a platter of half-eaten meatballs behind her, made her hope Blue Suit didn't think she was the greedy girl responsible. It was all Andrea's handiwork.

'Now then, Michael, this is Amanda. Michael Daniels meet Amanda. She works for Nora our Head of Litigation; you met

Nora at the luncheon today.' Michael nodded giving Andrea a friendly smile as Moira willed him to look her way once more. She wanted to be pinned under his gaze. She rolled his name around in her head imagining herself whispering it in his ear and then she went a step further, trying out Moira Daniels for size.

'It's Andrea, Mr Price.'

Fusty Pants cleared his throat. 'Quite right, of course it is. My apologies, let's start again, shall we? Michael, this is Anna and this lovely young woman here is Moira. She's one half of the duo on our front desk. It's her pretty face that will greet you each morning.' He gave her a lascivious once over.

Oh, feck off you old perve, he really was stuck in the seventies, Moira thought, giving Michael, whose eyes twinkled seeming to tell her he had Fusty Pants pegged, her most beatific and beguiling smile as she took his outstretched hand. For the briefest of seconds, she thought he was going to raise it to his lips and she had to force herself to stay upright and not curtsey. *Get a grip, Moira.*

She flirted outrageously by refusing to be the first to lower her eyes which were locked into his. For his part, he held her hand a tad too long. If Ciara from catering had returned with the platter of cocktail sausages on sticks she'd breezed past with a few moments earlier, Moira knew she would have taken one and made an unashamed show of herself nibbling on it. A crude thought she knew, but there was something about this man that was making her so.

Fusty Pants droned on about how fortunate they were to have Michael on board and how he and his family had relocated from London. He would officially be joining Mason Price as Partner in the Aviation and Asset Finance Department as of Monday. Two things lodged in Moira's befuddled consciousness as Michael finally dropped her hand. The first being that that explained why she hadn't seen him around the place—he wasn't due to start work until Monday. The second and more important point being that Fusty Pants had referred to a family. She sought his left hand for confirmation as to the definition of what a family might mean. It was thrust inside his suit pocket hidden from view. She cast around for conversation not wanting him to be dragged away just yet, finally dredging up, 'How is our fair city treating you so far then, Michael?'

He smiled and she very nearly swooned, glad she was holding onto the side of the table she was leaning up against.

'What's the phrase you Irish use when things are going well?' He might have been London based but his accent had the rounded vowels of someone whose roots were in the north of England.

'Grand.'

'Dublin's grand, tanks, Moira.' He dropped the 'h' in a poor imitation of the Irish accent.

Fusty Pants laughed as though he'd said something exceedingly witty before hauling Michael on his way to where the gaggle of Banking girls were waiting their turn.

'Jaysus, Moira, the two of you needed to get a room. The sexual tension between you.' She flapped her hand across her face, 'hot!'

'Do you think he's married? Fusty Pants mentioned a family.'

'Sadly, my guess is yes. He'll be what, in his late thirties?'

Moira nodded.

'Definitely married then, sorry, Moira, but he's too fecking gorgeous not to be. You know as well as I do, how it goes, the good ones are always snapped up early on. So, if I were you, I'd go to the Ladies, splash some cold water on your face and re-focus your affections on Liam Shaugnessy as per the plan you hatched at lunchtime today and I shall go dazzle Connor with my witty repartee.'

'Liam?'

'Yes, Asset Management Liam over there by Mary from Litigation who looks like she's about to attach herself to him like a limpet. Once she's latched on, he won't be able to get her off.'

Moira looked over at Liam. It was true she'd been making eyes at him this last while but she was ruined. Michael Daniels had ruined her for any other men—yes it was a dramatic thought but it was how she felt. The moment he'd caught her eye across the room, it was as though she'd been struck by lightning. All very clichéd but an accurate description nonetheless. Liam, she thought shooting him a second glance, came a sad second to Michael Daniels. Michael was a man, Liam a mere boy and Mary could have him. Just like a much-anticipated chocolate, unwrapped, and bitten into only to discover a nut in the middle, he'd lost his allure.

Michael turned and glanced over his shoulder locking eyes with Moira once more, and she felt herself begin to fall.

Chapter 7

Tessa Delaney nibbled her toast. She was mouse-like in the dainty way in which she was holding the triangle, savouring each small mouthful with its miserly scraping of marmalade. She'd opted for O'Mara's Continental breakfast this morning and had enjoyed a bowl of cereal with a dollop of yogurt, a treat given she was on holiday, before sliding her bread under the grill. One slice would suffice; anymore would be greedy, she'd told herself, tempting as it was. The marmalade, she was guessing, was homemade and it was delicious. It had taken all her willpower not to slather it on.

She knew the cook, Mrs Flaherty as she'd introduced herself when she'd approached her yesterday morning, had been perturbed by her previous day's breakfast order. It was why she'd opted for Continental today. Yesterday she'd asked for one egg to be served over easy on a slice of wholegrain toast, nothing strange in that. It was the omission of all the cook's lovingly fried trimmings, the bacon, sausage, and white pudding that had disconcerted the older woman. Tessa knew this because she recognised something in her as she stood with her arms clasped around her generous middle, a frown embedded on her forehead.

Mrs Flaherty was a feeder just like Tessa's mum. Her way of showing she cared had always been to pile her husband and daughter's plates sky high. Tessa had learned a long time ago to be firm, to not give in to the wounded look like the one plastered to Mrs Flaherty's face as she'd asked, *The white pudding's really rather good you know. I source only the best sweetbreads and are you sure I can't offer you a rasher on the side?*

Now, as she finished the last bite of her toast, she sensed movement out of the corner of her eye. A quick glance across to where it had come from near the entrance to the kitchen revealed it was Mrs Flaherty. She was waving her arms about as though in the throes of an energetic aerobics class. By the looks of it, she was engaging in a heated, one-sided conversation with Aisling, the establishment's manageress. Tessa couldn't hear what was being said in its entirety, their voices drowned by the clatter of knives and forks and general chatter from the other dining room occupants. She did, however, catch snippets of the words, *fecking and fox*, more than once. A strange conversation but it did explain the crash she'd heard outside her window in the middle of the night as she'd tried to get used to being in yet another strange bed. The culprit was obviously a fox getting into the bins on the hunt for scraps.

She didn't ponder the conversation further because her mind was otherwise occupied and her eyes swung to the clock on the wall near the dining room entrance. She did the maths, it was only nine hours until the ten-year school reunion of the pupils of St Mary's Secondary School in Blackrock. Nine short hours until she'd see Rowan Duffy, the bully who'd made her life, for what was ultimately only a short while in the grand scheme of things but at the time had seen interminable, almost unbearable. The wounds Rowan and her two awful friends had so carelessly inflicted hadn't been physical but Tessa still bore the scars of the taunts they'd tossed her way throughout her thirteenth year. She'd been unable to shake Rowan the ringleader—her nemesis had been with her ever since. The teenage spectre had clung on and become the whispering voice of self-doubt.

At the thought of what lay ahead that evening, her stomach turned over, a churning cocktail of nerves, excitement, and anticipation. She'd been waiting thirteen long years for tonight to roll around. It was thirteen years since she'd left Dublin and she'd been approaching the end of her thirteenth year at the time—half her lifetime ago. What was it about the number thirteen? It was supposed to be unlucky. Certainly, that year had been like the Queen famously once said, *annus horribilis,* but then one day, like a lighthouse beacon on a stormy night, her parents had offered her a way out.

The news that the family was to emigrate to New Zealand saw her set about reinventing herself. Once it had sunk in, she'd put her hand over her plate much to her mother's bewilderment, when she tried to ply her with a second helping. She'd gone without the lashings of butter she was partial to on her toast and cakes were off limits.

Her parents fretted and worried at first over her losing weight, putting it down to the impending move and unhappiness over leaving her friends. There'd been no time however in the flurry of packing their lives up to delve too deeply and in the end, they'd left Tessa alone. Her weight loss it was decided was due to the stress of moving and hormones. 'Sure,' she'd overheard her mother say to her father, 'aren't teenage girls supposed to be a mystery?' Through sheer bloody mindedness she'd arrived in New Zealand twenty pounds lighter and had never looked back until now.

She poured milk from the jug into her cup of tea, stirring it as she looked around the basement dining room. It was an elegant but functional space; in bygone days this would have been the servants' domain, she figured. The tables were laid with white cloths and set with silver cutlery. On the walls were various black and white prints of Dublin through the years. Her eyes settled on a shot of Grafton Street; judging by the street fashion it was taken in the twenties. A different world altogether she thought, sipping from her cup.

She turned her attention to her fellow guests, an eclectic bunch. There was an older couple each engrossed and apparently thoroughly enjoying the food in front of them. They'd be sure to get brownie points from Mrs Flaherty, she mused. A young couple were coaxing a small child who was vehemently shaking his head, into having another bite of his toast. If they weren't careful, they'd have a full-scale tantrum on their hands she thought, recognising the warning signs from her many nights spent babysitting. It had helped pay her way through university.

Her gaze fixed on the man she'd noticed at breakfast the previous morning. She'd seen him again when she dropped her key in at reception before heading out for a day's tripping down memory lane. It had amused her to see the receptionist, Bronagh, batting her lashes at him and talking in a girly voice. She was old enough to be his mother, but each to their own, she'd thought. One thing Tessa made sure she never did was sit in judgment of others.

She watched as he simultaneously sipped his tea and checked his Blackberry. A man who could multitask, now there was a sight to behold! He was clean-shaven, dressed for business not sight-seeing, and there was a shine on his shoes that would make any mother proud. She liked a man who took pride in his appearance, especially given how hard she worked to maintain her own. He looked to be around thirty at a guess and given the intensity of his frown she wondered what he had planned for the day. Was he brokering a make-or-break deal, or perhaps applying for a job in a career he'd been climbing the ladder toward since leaving school?

What would he think if he knew what her reasons were for coming back to Dublin after all this time? It was, after all, a long way to come for a high school reunion, especially given she'd only attended the school for a year. He'd think her strange, a little obsessed perhaps. She wondered if he'd read Stephen King's Carrie, because she knew the story would spring to mind. Her motives for coming back to Dublin weren't vengeful though. Oh, she couldn't deny it was going to be satisfying to see the look of shock on Rowan and the rest of her motley crew's faces when they saw how she'd turned out. She'd show them she'd succeeded despite them. Although, sometimes she wondered if her drive to be the best version of herself in every aspect of her life was *because* of them.

It was something she'd played out in her mind over and over again these last few months since she'd booked her plane ticket. She'd left *Ten Tonne Tessie* behind in Dublin when she and her parents left all those years ago. These days she was Tessa Delaney, Ms, by the way— that she was single was nobody's business but her own. A svelte Investment Consultant for a leading Auckland finance company with a personal assistant and an office overlooking the city and out to sea. She could see as far as the extinct volcano, Rangitoto Island, on a clear day.

Her home was a restored villa with a red pohutukawa tree in the garden with a slash of blue ocean visible from her living room window. She'd grown used to watching the sea with its ever-changing moods and would find it hard not to have it in her line of sight. The villa had two spare bedrooms; it seemed she'd also inherited her mother's penchant for houses that were too big for their small family.

She'd kept in touch with her old school pal, Saoirse, over the years. They'd updated one another with the way their lives were panning out in the form of letters winging their way back and forth two, three times a year. Tessa would have liked to have come over for her friend's wedding but she'd been angling for promotion at the time and couldn't ask for time off. Saoirse would mention too from time to time that she'd love to bring her family out for a holiday in New Zealand, but financially, with young children and an enormous mortgage, it wasn't on the cards.

She told Tessa things from time to time. Like how she wished she'd been made of sterner stuff and had been able to stand up for her friend back when they were at St Mary's. Tessa told her she wasn't to blame, it wasn't up to Saoirse to sort her problems out. She should have had the sense to talk to her mother about what was happening to her. Hindsight was a wonderful thing and the choices her sensible adult self would make were very different to her frightened childhood self.

Saoirse would tell her things in her letters too, like how the only skill Rowan had learned during her schooling was how to light a cigarette on a windy day—a talent fine honed down the back of the school field. She'd been expelled at sixteen for one misdemeanour too many. Saoirse would mention how she'd seen her from afar on a trip to Dublin and how it seemed she had an ongoing penchant for wearing her skirts too short. The last she'd heard of her, she was working in a café. Tessa had felt just the teensiest bit gleeful as she'd read that it wasn't even one of the posh new cafés springing up about the city but a right old greasy spoon.

It was also Saoirse who'd mentioned the reunion. She'd written that the ten-year reunion of St Mary's class of 1989 was being held in the school hall this October and how she had no intention of going. For one thing, she lived in Galway these days and for another, there was nobody she was particularly interested in reuniting with! Tessa hadn't even been at the school in 1989 but it didn't matter. She knew as she sat reading and re-reading her friend's letter that she would be going. She'd talk Saoirse into going with her too because this was it, this was her chance for closure where Rowan and her two ugly stepsisters were concerned. It was her opportunity to confront her past and in doing so quieten that inner voice that still, even now governed how she felt others perceived her.

There were two Tessas—the outwardly confident version she'd perfected the moment she'd begun her new life in Herne Bay, Auckland and the Tessa who lived on inside her. The fearful, frightened Tessa who wasn't worthy of being loved.

Tessa blinked, she hadn't realised the man had looked up, bemused no doubt by the intensity of her stare. He was smiling at her and she glanced away, embarrassed at being caught out, feeling the pull to the past as she stepped back into 1987.

Chapter 8

1987

TESSA BURST THROUGH the front door of the large, too large for the three of them, detached house overlooking the sea where they lived in a leafy Blackrock Street. Mummy had always wanted a detached house, no matter that two of the four bedrooms remained empty and two bathrooms meant two bathrooms that needed to be cleaned each week—Tessa's loathed pocket-money job.

She'd slammed the door shut behind her not caring if she got told off and, resting her back against it, she willed her heart to stop racing. It was only then when she could feel the solid timber separating her from the outside world did she feel safe to let the tears that had threatened all the way home spill over.

'We're in the kitchen, Tessa darling.' Her mother's voice tinkled down the hall with no hint of reproach over her heavy handedness with the front door. Tessa swiped at her cheeks. She wouldn't let her see she was upset. It wouldn't do any good telling her what was going on. She'd only get a name for herself as a tattle-tale at school which would give Rowan and her gang of two more ammunition. She had thought about confiding in Sister Evangelista when she'd asked her if everything was alright last week. Tessa's overly bright eyes and flushed cheeks hadn't escaped her kindly, eagle eyes, but sure, what could the nun do? She sniffed knowing there was nothing for it but to keep ignoring them in the hope they'd get bored and leave her be.

It was only a ten-minute walk from the school gates to her front door but it was a journey that could be fraught with as much danger as navigating the Serengeti Plains on foot. They'd been learning about Africa in class that morning and as she'd stared down at the picture in the book Sister Mary Leo had passed around with its glossy photographs, Tessa had felt a kinsman ship with the beleaguered impala. Rowan, Teresa, and Vicky reminded her of the pack of wild dogs their teeth bared, caught on film as they hunted the poor creature.

She could avoid Rowan and the other two at lunchtime by taking herself off to the library with her friend, Saoirse, who was, if anything, even more timid than she was but Saoirse wasn't fat. There wasn't much of anything that stood out about Saoirse, she blended in with the crowd so they left her alone. It was as the clock on the classroom wall ticked its way ever closer to the final bell that the panic would begin to set in. Tessa would find herself unable to concentrate on her lesson as her heart beat a little faster, her breath sticking in her throat as the sick feeling in the pit of her stomach amped up. It was the worry, she knew this, whether the day would be a good day. She'd cross her fingers, the skin around her nails red from being nibbled at, under the desk and promise extra Hail Marys if today could please be a good day.

A good day was when she managed to race out the school gates and put a decent distance between herself and the trio lying in wait. Today she thought, her head still resting against the front door, hadn't been a good day. Sister Geraldine had continued to drone on, obviously enthralled with the particular period in history she was informing her students of, and Tessa had felt like screaming. She'd wanted to stand up and yell at the nun, 'I don't give a flying feck about the Battle of the Boyne. I care about those ganky cows who'll all be waiting for me at the gate if you don't shut up and let me go home!'

Of course, she hadn't said a word. She'd sat at her desk clenching her fists so that the ragged ends of her nails dug into her palms. The seconds had ticked over into minutes and around her, her classmates had begun to fidget in their eagerness to be excused for the day. Still, Sister Geraldine waffled on. Tessa's gaze had flicked anxiously between the clock and the door until at last Sister Geraldine reached the part where King James II of England fled to France never to be seen in Ireland again. It was at this point Sister Geraldine gave the signal that they were allowed to slam their history books shut. There was a collective thudding as the heavy tomes were closed, followed by a mass scraping of chairs as the girls pushed past one another eager for the off.

As Tessa slid her bag's straps over her shoulders, she'd felt a small surge of hope. It was nearly ten past; surely they'd have tired of waiting for her and headed home by now. She'd walk extra slow so as to be sure to give them a head start. A few beats later her heart sank as she stepped outside and saw them milling about by the entrance. They'd elbowed each other as she came into sight. Their skirts were worn short enough for the nuns to frown upon and make noises about telling their mothers to unpick the hems, but long enough for them to be generally left alone. School ties had been loosened and socks were puddled around ankles. Tessa knew too that as soon as the bell had rung, their bags would have been hastily opened to retrieve stacks of multi-coloured jelly bracelets stashed at the bottom. These were then layered up their wrists in a school girl homage to Madonna for the walk home.

Tessa had looked straight ahead pretending she couldn't see them as she passed through the gates and out onto the street. If she pretended hard enough, surely they'd vanish. She made a silent phffing noise as she imagined them disappearing like a puff of smoke. She didn't even wince when Rowan called out in a voice designed to carry.

'Ooh lookout, girls, there she goes, Ten Tonne Tessie. Can you feel the ground shaking, Terry?'

Tessa had heard the snapping of gum and giggling.

'Fi, fi, fo fum, by gum, Tessa's got a big bum.'

'I can hear her thighs rubbing together from here!'

Titters and more gum popping.

Onwards she'd trudged, her eyes trained to the ground in front of her. One foot being placed in front of the other. Plodding, solid steps, befitting the solid, plodding lump she was. Her eyes burned and she blinked furiously, she would not let them know she heard them or that she cared what they thought. She pulled on her imaginary coat of armour and fended the taunts off like they were arrows—they were useless against her iron defence shield as they pinged off her and hit the ground.

It hadn't protected her from the pebble that hit her squarely in the back. 'Oi, we're talking to you, fat girl.'

'Tessa, is that you, love?'

Her mother's voice brought her back and she swiped her nose before calling, 'Yes, I'm coming, Mum.'

She pushed herself away from the door and, dumping her bag at the foot of the stairs to take up to her room later, she padded down the hall to the kitchen. It was her favourite room in the house. It looked out on the garden and to the sea and there were always comforting smells emanating from it. Her nose twitched at the aroma of something sugary and soft with a hint of spice and her tummy rumbled in anticipation. 'Hello,' she said, a flash of fear passing through her at the sight of Dad sitting at the table. He was in his suit which meant he'd been to work but he didn't usually get home until five o'clock. What was going on? She felt that familiar quickening of her heart and the sick feeling in her stomach. Nora Heatherington's father had been laid off last week and Nora said her parents had been doing a lot of shouting and whispering but not much proper talking ever since. She was reassured a little by his smile. He did not look like a man who'd received bad news. Mum, she noticed was wearing her new top, the one with the sparkles along the neckline that she'd helped her choose. Surely, she wouldn't be wearing a pretty sparkly top if something awful had happened.

'Hello, Tessa love, come on, sit down,' her mum said, patting her place at the table. 'I'll butter you a nice slice of brack.'

She sat down quickly.

In the middle of the table was the source of the aroma that had beckoned her in; a plate stacked with slices of fresh fruity, brack. Her mum smeared thick butter on the piece she'd put on a plate for Tessa and slid it across the table to where she sat. Tessa's gaze swung anxiously from one parent to the other.

'You're probably wondering why Daddy's home?'

She hated it when Mum called Dad, Daddy. She wasn't a baby but now wasn't the time to protest and she nodded because her mouth was too full to speak. She'd shovelled in as much of the loaf as she could fit, hoping it would quell the un-settled feeling that had descended the moment she stepped in-to the kitchen—homemade brack fixed most things especially when it had extra raisins in it.

'Well, Daddy and I, we've got some news. We think it's very exciting and we hope you do too.'

She was all ears.

'A grand opportunity's come our way. Daddy—'

Tessa wondered if they'd rehearsed this, whatever this was, as her dad cleared his throat and Mum picked up the knife to butter a second slice of loaf for Tessa.

'What it is, Tess,' her father continued. 'I've been offered a job in New Zealand. Auckland to be precise. It seems they need civil engineers there.'

Tessa's mouth fell open despite its contents—New Zealand! 'Are you taking it?'

'Tessa, finish your mouthful first.' Her mother frowned across the table ever mindful of manners.

She did so knowing she'd get the hiccups from eating too fast. 'Sorry,' she said after swallowing, feeling the loaf sitting solid like a lump of coal in her throat. 'But, New Zealand? Mum, Dad that's the other side of the world.'

They didn't seem fazed by her shock. If anything their eyes flickered with amusement. 'We know where it is.' They smiled at each other and Tessa wanted to throw the piece of loaf her mother had now put on her plate at them. They weren't making any sense. You didn't just decide to move to New Zealand. It wasn't Cork or Galway or even the UK for that matter. It was about as far away from Ireland, her home, as you could go. And why hadn't they discussed any of this with her?

'It probably seems like a bolt from the blue to you, love.'

She nodded so furiously she felt at risk of dislocating her neck.

'*It is* rather sudden we know, but the opportunity for Daddy to put in for a transfer arose and we'd only ever heard wonderful things about New Zealand. We didn't want to say anything until it was definite in case it all fell through.'

It was definite, her mum had just said it was definite.

'And, Tessa, I'm always after telling you that to be successful in life you need to embrace opportunities and be open to change.'

It was true, she was always saying stupid stuff like that. She meant it to be encouraging and inspiring but mostly when she said it, it was annoying. Tessa's lips formed a mutinous line that caused her mum to babble on.

'Take my old school friend, Naomi, for example. She moved to New Zealand years ago when she got married—he was from there, her husband. She still sends me a Christmas card and her life in—' she looked to her husband for help.

'Christchurch,' Dad obliged.

'Christchurch sounds marvellous. In summer it's an endless round of picnics and barbecues. They live outdoors in New Zealand.'

What was her mother saying? They'd sleep under the stars? She wasn't selling her on the idea if that was the case. Tessa did not like camping. Her one and only experience had been with the Brownies. The heavens had opened and they'd all had to take cover. It had been the stuff of nightmares with Brown Owl trying to jolly them all along as they huddled together shivering.

'Then there's the Joyce family. You won't remember them, they lived a few doors down from us when you were a baby. They moved, all seven of them, to the capital.'

This time it was Tessa who piped up, breaking a piece of brack off with her fingers, the word tripping automatically from her tongue. 'Wellington,' she said, popping the morsel in her mouth. She'd learned a little about New Zealand in her geography lessons at school. She'd also learned it was a country that sat on the Ring of Fire. It had volcanos; most of them were extinct but you never knew *and* it was prone to earthquakes.

Mum took this as an encouraging sign. 'Yes, Wellington, and the last time I heard they were living in a great big house, overlooking the sea.'

A great big house seemed to matter a great big deal to her mother, Tessa thought. 'Our house is big and it overlooks the sea.' She knew her tone was belligerent.

This time her mother didn't tell her to finish her mouthful before speaking. Her eyes flitted nervously across the table to her husband. She wasn't giving them the response they'd been hoping for. He came to her rescue.

'Ah, but in Auckland where we're going, its warmer, almost tropical, and you'll be able to swim all summer long without catching hypothermia. You can eat watermelon every day too if you like.'

This Tessa knew had been tossed in because she'd developed a fondness for slices of the sweet fruit when it had been served up for breakfast on their all-inclusive holiday to Florida when she was nine.

Mum flashed him a grateful look but Tessa was only half listening now as her mind tried to wrap itself around this bombshell news. The word definite reverberated in her ears. Further evidence of their seriousness was in the nervous darting glances Mum kept shooting at Dad. She could tell too that they were holding hands under the table—moral support. They didn't think she knew they did this. It made her feel pitted against the odds, two against one. 'You said it's definite.' Her voice was flat.

It was their turn to nod and she was pleased to see they had the grace to look a little shame-faced at having made such a momentous decision without consulting her. Two against one, she thought once more. 'When? When will we go?'

'Just short of three months. I know it seems sudden, but this way we can have a good long holiday and settle in properly before you begin your new school. It will be their summer holidays so you won't start until the February. Imagine, Tessa you'll be sunbathing and swimming while everyone here will be in their winter woollies sniffing with coughs and colds. And, sure it's not as though you've been at St Mary's for years. You'll settled into your new school no bother.'

How would she know? Tessa pushed her chair back and ran from the room. She couldn't comprehend it and she couldn't take another second of their anxious expressions willing her to jump for joy at what they'd just laid on her. She heard her mum get up to follow her and Dad's voice saying, 'Leave her, Sheelagh. She needs some time by herself to get used to the idea. We knew it'd come as a shock to her.'

She took the stairs two at a time and threw herself down on her bed. She lay there staring at the ceiling and the boys from Duran Duran stared down at her from the poster she'd sellotaped above her bed. 'Can you believe it, John?' she whispered. John Taylor was her favourite band member, he had the most soulful of brown eyes and always looked like he understood when she confided in him. 'New Zealand. They want to drag me all the way to New Zealand. They've gone mad, the pair of them.' It was times like this Tessa hated being an only child. If she had an ally, things wouldn't seem so bad. Two against two.

She folded her arms across her chest and it was then it dawned on her. Her eyes widened because she herself had just said—it was the other side of the world. There would be no Rowan Duffy in Auckland. No Vicky, no Teresa. On the other side of the world, she wouldn't be Ten Tonne Tessie, she'd be Tessa Delaney, newly arrived from Ireland. She could be exotic, like Audrey from Paris, who'd spent the first term this year at St Mary's. All the girls had wanted to be friends with her simply because she was different—in a good way, not a fat way. The more she mulled it over the more she warmed to the idea. She was being given a clean slate. She could start over and suddenly, moving to the Southern Hemisphere seemed no bad thing at all.

Chapter 9

Michael was on Moira's mind and as a result, she was tossing and turning, getting tangled in her sheets. She hated the fact she was alone in her bed; that he couldn't stay here with her. She didn't like to think about what his life was like at home. It was something she tried to store in the out-of-bounds compartment. It was where she stored the worst of her pain, her memories of her daddy's last days were tucked away in there too. Her mind, however, was a law unto itself and tonight it wouldn't stop straying there, determined to pick over all the details she'd filed away like an efficient secretary regarding Michael.

She knew he'd chosen to buy in Sandy Cove and he lived in the house they'd purchased with his wife and two children. The postcode meant their home would be expensive, more than likely detached, and for some reason she kept picturing an enormous rumpus room. 'Rumpus room,' she rolled the words off her tongue in a whisper, it sounded posh. There'd be no sitting on top of one another in a poky front room for the Daniels family, not in Sandy Cove.

His girls, he'd told her the first time they'd sat and talked, had started at a nearby private school. He'd looked pleased as he told her they'd settled into their new lives here in Dublin well. It was something that had clearly bothered him about making the move, given their awkward ages. He'd also confided they were the reason he stayed with his wife. The marriage, he'd told her earnestly, had been over for years but they'd agreed to do their best by their girls. They owed them that and their best meant staying together until the children both finished their schooling. It would be too disruptive, too selfish not to. Their happiness had to come before his. There'd been something in his eyes that had willed her to understand the situation he found himself duty bound to.

She'd felt a tug, her heart going out to him for the situation he found himself in. He was a good man, she thought. Despite what Andrea had told her when she'd heard what he'd had to say. 'That's the sort of thing all married men say to young women they want to cop off with. It doesn't make you special, Moira. Don't believe a word of it.' Moira had been annoyed because she knew Michael wasn't like most married men. She'd replied, 'But you weren't there. You didn't see the look on his face when he talked about his marriage. He looked trapped, desperate almost.' His eyes had begged her to understand and he had beautiful eyes.

'You're being played.' Andrea had rolled her eyes and shaken her head. It was the first time Moira had contemplated falling out with her friend but somehow, she'd bitten back a retort because she knew if the shoe were on the other foot, she'd be saying the same thing to her.

Michael's oldest daughter was fifteen and the youngest had recently turned thirteen. They weren't babies by any means, but she also knew what she'd been like as a teenager—independent yet fully dependent at the same time. A woman/child. She'd needed her mam and dad every bit as much as she'd protested she didn't. At a time of uncertainty and change, not to mention mood swings, they'd been her constant. Parents, she thought her eyes wide in the dark, should be like a solid brick wall. No matter how hard you pushed against them they remained there, solid. It was what made it so hard to accept her Daddy wasn't here anymore. Half her wall had crumbed down.

It wasn't too late to walk away. She could leave Michael to weather his marriage out to the end. It wasn't like they'd done more than talk and exchange a few kisses. She flexed her hand in the darkness imagining she could feel the solid warmth of his in it. There was no chance of them exchanging more than a few polite words at work and other than a few stolen hours over the course of these last few weeks their time was very much not their own. Despite this, she'd fallen for him.

He'd made his choices. She didn't need to be involved in them. She knew the reason Andrea had annoyed her was because she was right, in so much as she should step back. The problem was what she should do and what she wanted to do were two very different beasts. 'You're playing with fire, Moira,' Andrea warned the last time Moira had mentioned Michael's name. At the same time though, Moira knew her friend well enough to see she was on the edge of her seat waiting for the next instalment. *She* was on the edge of her seat waiting, too. She had been from the moment he'd cupped her face in his hands and kissed her. She hadn't seen it coming and she'd tried to pull away, but truth be told she hadn't tried very hard.

He'd confessed after that first kiss, he'd been unable to stop thinking about her since the night he'd seen her across the boardroom. She'd gotten under his skin, he said. The rest of the staff he'd greeted had paled and blurred after Noel Price introduced him to her. He'd not been able to get the impossible green and gold of her eyes out of his head. Moira sighed, her breath warm against the chill of the room. The central heating had clicked off hours ago. She couldn't wait five long years for them to be together properly. Her throat constricted as the thought of the days, weeks, and months stretching into years of what her sister would call furtive behaviour filled her with panic. She didn't want to be that girl. How had she got here? It was a pointless question, she knew exactly how she'd gotten here.

Chapter 10

How it began...

The poster in the window caught Moira's eyes and she came to a standstill. Standing in the shop frontage, huddled inside her coat she was oblivious to the corporate clad women who nearly walked into her. The woman sidestepped her at the last minute with a muttered, 'for feck's sake,' barely faltering in her frantic pace.

Moira was on her way home from work, in no great hurry to get there either given it was a Tuesday and nothing much happened at home on a Tuesday. Aisling was likely to while away her evening distracting Quinn in the kitchen of his bistro and it was her least favourite night on the television. She was too broke to suggest an impromptu night out to see a film or have a meal with Andrea. It would be a waste of time, anyway. Andrea was devoted to her soaps, Moira loved hers too but preferred to curl up on the sofa of a weekend, snacks to hand, to watch the omnibus on offer. At the very least it would take a Brad Pitt film to drag Andrea away from her viewing and, so far as Moira knew, he wasn't starring in anything at the Savoy this week.

So, there she was standing on the pavement outside the Baggot Street, Boots staring at the image of Elizabeth Hurley on display. The glossy poster was marketing at its best she mused, wrestling with the should she or shouldn't she question.

Liz, all ethereal and lovely, boasted of a serum containing the latest miracle properties—it was packaged in a simple, sleek silver bottle. Her Visa card, with which she had a love- hate relationship, burned a hole in her pocket.

Serum, the word whispered to her, and Moira decided she liked the way it sounded. It wasn't quite on a par with conniption but it did sound exotic and full of promise. What the poster didn't mention though was what the undoubtedly eye-watering price for the magical properties contained in the silver cannister was. But sure, what price did you put on a miracle? She asked herself torn between a magical serum or the bottle of Allure—the new Chanel fragrance she'd had a spray of the last time she'd been in the chemist. She was nearly out of perfume. *What to do, what to do?* She was too busy wrestling with her dilemma to realise someone was standing alongside her until they cleared their throat.

'Moira, hi. I like your shoes.'

She hoped she didn't look like a total eejit as her mouth fell open and she wished she wasn't standing in front of such an enormous photo of Elizabeth Hurley as she gawped up at Michael Daniels. No woman could compete with Liz when she was doing provocative, and why oh why wasn't she in her heels all glamorous instead of her runners? She looked like Minnie Mouse. She gathered herself quickly as her heart began to hammer and her stomach danced to a fluttering beat. 'Ah well, now, Mr Daniels, I can't very well be trotting home in my stilettos now can? How're you settling in at Mason Price?'

He grinned and his smile lit his eyes. He had lovely teeth she thought randomly as she reminded herself to blink.

'Very sensible of you. The shoes I mean, although you do realise I'm going to have to start calling you Minnie Mouse.'

What was he she thought, a mind reader?

'And I am settling in thanks even if the weather has been awful since we arrived. But please don't call me Mr Daniels it makes me feel like my father! It's Michael, Moira. So, are you contemplating a spot of shopping or are you on your way home?'

We, she realised her heart plummeting, he'd used *we*. 'Both, and I probably shouldn't be contemplating the shopping. I should be saving for a deposit.'

He raised an eyebrow.

'For a flat, I live just across from the Green, in O'Mara's Guesthouse with my sister.'

'A guesthouse, that sounds interesting.'

Moira shrugged, she'd gotten used to people's curiosity when they realised she lived on the top floor of a busy, established old guesthouse. It wasn't the norm, but it was her norm. 'It's home. Well kind of, our mammy moved out recently and it's just me and my sister rattling around there these days. Aisling, that's my sister manages the place. We rub along alright so long as she doesn't tell me what I should be doing, but I'd still like my own place. It's not on the cards for a while though, not with rents being sky high and flats being so hard to come by.' She hoped she wasn't babbling. She was unused to the effect being in his presence was having on her, she was the girl who always played it cool.

'Supply and demand.' He gave her a rueful grin and her knees threatened to give way. She realised she'd zoned out the hordes of people buzzing past them when a man apologised for knocking Michael's shoulder.

'Well, it's a miserable evening and I'm sure you don't want to spend it standing around on the street talking to me! I'd better let you get on home. It was good seeing you, Moira.'

'Oh, I'm not in a hurry.' The short sentence popped forth unbidden, a bold invitation to talk longer.

That smile again and a slight hesitation. Moira looked at Michael expectantly. For his part, his expression was one of surprise but then he smiled again and rubbed his jawline; she could see the beginnings of a five o'clock shadow. 'Well, if you're not in a rush, then it would be great to get the low-down on my new hometown from a local. You know where to go, where not to go, that sort of thing. We could grab a drink, have a bite to eat? My treat.'

'Don't you have to get home?' She regretted the words as soon as she'd said them but she'd definitely heard that *we*.

It was like the sun went in behind the clouds. 'No, I'm not in a rush either but I didn't mean to put you on the spot so, if you'd rather not—'

Moira jumped in, 'You didn't. There's a pub not far from here, The Iron Bridge, they do a deadly Boxty if you're keen to try something traditional. We could call in there if you like?'

'I'd like that.'

They smiled at each other, pleased with the arrangement, and merged in with the tide of people walking up the street. 'Deadly Boxty?' he said a beat later, keeping pace with her. 'It sounds like some sort of mushroom. Should I be worried?'

Moira laughed. 'Boxty's an Irish staple, they're potato pancakes and where I'm taking you, they're served with a lemon and chive mayonnaise.' Under normal circumstances, Moira's mouth would have watered at the thought of the crispy, golden pancakes but this situation was anything but normal. She was too aware of Michael's proximity, hypersensitive to the brush of his arm against hers.

She spied Quinn's Bistro ahead and quickened her pace, casting a sideways glance as they passed by the cheery red door with its welcoming brass nameplate above it. Inside, she knew would be warm and inviting. The roaring open fire set back in the wall of exposed bricks would beckon people to sit down and take a load off. The low timber-beamed ceiling added to the cosiness and the atmosphere would be convivial and bustling. This would have been a great spot to introduce Michael to. Quinn's had a bar, live music, the food was great and so was the craic, but she wasn't risking bumping into Aisling. She didn't want her sister giving Michael the third degree as to who he was and what his intentions were. The odds of her sister being there at this time of the evening were slim but Moira's luck had never been great and even if she wasn't there, Alasdair the maître d' would be sure to pass on the news he'd seen Moira with a mystery man.

The thing was, she wasn't sure how she'd explain Michael if she were to bump into anybody she knew. It wasn't as if they were colleagues. They worked for the same firm, yes, but he held a senior position and ne'er the twain do mix. It was a sort of unwritten rule. Her step faltered, what was she doing? She was ninety per cent sure Michael was married and a man who was spoken for shouldn't be going for a drink with the receptionist at the law firm he worked at.

Her mammy's face flashed before her, with the same expression she'd had picking up Moira from school the day she'd gotten caught smoking in the girls' toilets. *Oh, go away, Mammy*, she gave her a mental shove and eyed Michael from under her lashes. There was still a ten per cent chance he was single. She was prepared to take a gamble even if the odds weren't good. Besides, she wasn't doing anything wrong. A drink, that's all it was. They were going for a drink not hotfooting it into the nearest hotel and asking for a room. As they reached the lights, the wind gusted down the road nearly cutting her in half, the sudden chill a welcome distraction from her thoughts.

'That's straight off the polar circle,' Michael muttered, shoving his hands deeper into his coat pockets. Moira nodded her agreement, shivering inside her coat as she wondered why, if it was all so innocent, she was so busy trying to justify her actions.

Chapter 11

The welcoming warmth from the blazing fire engulfed them as soon as they stepped inside The Iron Bridge. Michael shut the door after her, grateful to leave the chill wind outside and Moira smiled back at the barman who'd looked up from where he was pulling a pint to give them a welcoming grin. He was serving a middle-aged man and woman in the unmistakable casual clobber of cashed-up tourists.

The pub was busy given it was a Tuesday night and as Moira glanced around, she saw the majority of the patrons looked to be tourists, all after a taste of Guinness in an authentic Irish pub. Michael scanned the room and raising his eyebrows questioningly gestured to the only free table. It was in the far corner of the room by the stage. Moira saw there was a microphone and a stool in the middle of it but doubted there'd be live music tonight, and if there was, it wouldn't start until later. It would do nicely, and she nodded her agreement nearly tripping over the long stretched out legs of a man too busy loading his camera to notice her as she followed Michael over to it.

He pulled a chair out for her and helped her out of her coat. These were old-fashioned gestures the fellows she dated didn't bother with but which she'd observed her daddy do for her mammy many times. She liked it. It made her feel special she decided sitting down and waiting for him to drape his own wool coat over the back of his chair. He did so taking a moment to soak up the expansive use of timber throughout the cosy space, and the dim lighting of their surrounds before he sat down opposite her.

'There's no doubt about it, Moira, you Irish know how to do a good pub.'

Moira smiled pleased with her choice of venue.

'Now then, what can I get you to drink?'

'Well since we're being all traditional a pint of Guinness, please. The brewery's only down the road, you can do tours of it. You should put that on your list of things to do now you're in Dublin. You'll have seen the stacks?'

He nodded. 'I can't say I'm a stout man but when in Rome and all that.'

'That's the spirit.' Moira grinned. 'It's full of iron you know, it's a tonic more than a drink.' She said this tongue in cheek having experienced the morning after too much so-called tonic more than once. 'And my daddy always said it put hairs on your chest.'

'Did he now?' He looked amused getting up from his seat. Moira sat toying with a beer mat watching him make his way up to the bar. She itched to call Andrea and tell her where she was but she left her phone in her bag. There was no time for that; Michael was being served and he'd be back in a moment.

He returned with two pints both of which had a creamy head on them.

Moira picked hers up and held it toward him. 'Slàinte.'

He clinked his glass against hers.

'It's Gaelic for health. Now you say, slàinte agad-sa which means your health as well.' She looked at him expectantly.

'Slàinte agad-sa,' he repeated awkwardly, and Moira laughed.

'We'll make an Irish man of you yet.' They both took a sip, and she pointed to his upper lip as he put his glass down. 'That's the sign of a good pint, a Guinness moustache.'

He wiped it away with the back of his hand eyeing his glass. 'That's not bad, you know. Maybe it's a subconscious thing. It tastes better because I'm in Ireland.'

'Ah well now, pouring a Guinness is an art form and if it's not done properly you miss out on a lot of the flavours. I watched him, yer man behind the bar, and he knows how it's done. Slowly, that's the way. It can't be rushed.'

'You're very knowledgeable on the topic.'

'I'm Irish, aren't I?'

'You are indeed. Now, what about those potato pancakes you mentioned?'

'I'll get those.' She was up and out of her seat before he could protest. Her finances were not in good shape but she could stretch to two orders of Boxty. She didn't want to feel beholden to him in any way. She just wanted to sit and talk, get to know him a bit better and, she assured herself making her way up to the bar, there was nothing wrong in that.

When she returned, Michael asked her to tell him what it was like living above a guesthouse. She settled back in her seat enjoying the warmth that was settling over her both from the fire and the Guinness and began by telling him about the dumbwaiter. It ran from the basement kitchen, past the first, and second floors right up to their apartment. 'It was a great place to hide when I was in trouble with Mammy. If I could get in the thing—Aisling used to take herself off and sit in it reading. She's a bookworm, our Aisling and it was the best place to tuck herself away when she didn't feel like doing her chores.' She made him laugh filling him in on Idle Ita and Bronagh their receptionist who'd worked for the family so long she was a part of it. 'Bronagh's always on a diet, supposedly, but she has a permanent stash of custard cream biscuits in her top drawer she's forever eating her way through while blaming her belly on the menopause.'

'And you're the youngest you say?'

'I am, and the others never let me forget it. It can be very annoying. There's nine years between me and Aisling, then there's Rosie, and Patrick who's the oldest.' She gave him her parents backstory of how they'd taken over the running of the three-storey Georgian townhouse overlooking St Stephen's Green from her grandparents, who'd converted it into a guest-house many moons ago when the upkeep of the manor house got too much. 'A house like that always needs something fixing. It was the plumbing in one of the guest rooms this week. When Mammy and Daddy took over, it was tired, but Mammy set about doing the place up. It was a mammoth undertaking, but she has an eye for that sort of thing and they made a grand pair playing the convivial hosts. The guesthouse got a good name for itself. It's busy all year round although why anyone would want to come to Dublin this time of year is beyond me.'

'You said your mother moved out recently?' Michael asked, and Moira tried not to focus on the plain gold band in clear view as he raked his hair back with his fingers.

The sight of it threw her.

'Moira?'

'Erm, I did, sorry.' She forced herself to stop staring at the ring and meet his eyes. She saw the question in them. 'Everything changed after my daddy died.' Her voice caught.

'I'm sorry to hear that.'

'Thanks,' she managed to say over the golf ball sized lump that had formed in her throat. She didn't look up; her eyes were trained on the Guinness that had slid down the side of her glass to puddle on the table. She dabbed at it with a napkin as she tried to compose herself. 'It was cancer and it was the worst thing me, or any of our family have ever been through in our lives, watching Daddy waste away. He was always there for us, you know. He was like a big strong rock and none of us were ready to lose him. I still can't believe he's not here anymore.' She took a deep, steadying breath. 'It's part of why I'd like to move out and get a place of my own. I see him everywhere. It's why Mammy moved on. She said it was too hard living with his ghost and she didn't want to spend the rest of her days mouldering away in the guesthouse on her own.'

'I can understand that. I lost my dad a couple of years ago too and it was tough. Damned tough. He shaped every decision I ever made because I wanted to be just like him right from when I was a little lad. Then one day, he keeled over and that was that, he was gone. He'd had a massive coronary, no warning, nothing. It was a terrible shock.'

Moira looked up then and he reached across the table. His hand rested briefly on hers as he said, 'People tell you it gets easier.'

She nodded, it was a platitude she'd heard many times in the early days after Brian O'Mara's passing. 'They do, but I don't believe them.'

'It doesn't get easier. I don't think losing someone you love deeply ever can, I think what people mean is that the pain stops being raw. It's a bit like a scab healing over, that part heals but you're left with the scarring as a permanent reminder.'

Moira nodded, chewing her bottom lip. That, she could believe.

'It might sound crazy, Moira, but I believe my father's still with me. I feel him. I think he walks alongside me, watching over me and those that I love.'

'Like an angel.' It was a lovely sentiment, she hoped her daddy was with the angels.

Michael smiled, 'If you'd ever met him, you'd know it's hard to imagine him as an angel but yes, something like that.'

Moira felt something pass between them then as he held her gaze across the table. He understood her. He understood her pain. Nobody else did. She'd stopped talking to her sisters about the big black hole inside of her that she was frightened would consume her. They were moving on with their own lives. Aisling had Quinn, and Rosie, well Rosie had the chinless wonder and gorgeous Noah. Patrick was caught up in Patrick, and Mammy was always busy with all her different clubs and committees. And now she was off to fecking Vietnam! It was only her that seemed unable to get past her grief.

The arrival of the Boxty, golden and crunchy as promised, lightened the mood between them and Moira realised she was ravenous. They tucked in, making appreciative noises as to the deliciousness of the pancakes and the perfection of the lemon and chive mayonnaise they slathered them in.

'I'm sold,' Michael said, wiping his mouth with a napkin and pushing his chair back a little once they'd cleared their plates. 'Those were bloody fantastic. Another drink?'

Moira smiled hoping her mouth wasn't shiny with grease. 'Yes, please.' She was feeling very mellow in a happily satiated way.

'So, Moira O'Mara, tell me more about how you and your sister came to be in charge of the guesthouse,' Michael said, putting the foamy pints on the table and sitting down once more.

'Well, like I said, when Daddy died, Mammy couldn't face running O'Mara's on her own. She gave us an ultimatum. Either one of us take over the management of the guesthouse or she'd put it on the market. My oldest sister, Roisin, is married to a chinless eejit over in London; he was keen for it to be sold as was my brother Patrick. He's living in LA, he's very successful at whatever it is he does.' She waved her hand, 'He's an entrepreneur. I think he would have liked the guesthouse sold so he could free up some capital for investment. He wasn't very happy when Aisling stepped up and said she'd take over.' Moira paused, her drink halfway to her lips as she frowned at the memory. She adored Patrick even if he was proving to be a self-absorbed prick, and she hadn't liked the angst Aisling's decision had caused, but at the same time, she'd been secretly proud of her sister for sticking to her guns.

'You weren't keen to take over?'

Moira snorted and then flushed. 'Sorry, not very ladylike of me. But no, Aisling was the right person for the job. She's got a background in hospitality, she worked in resort management. I used to go pea-green over the places she was sent to. We'd get these postcards from the Whitsunday Islands in Australia, Fiji, the Seychelles. Places where the sun always seemed to be shining and the postman would always drop them in to us on miserable, rainy days. She was in Crete when she decided to pack it in and come home. Aisling's got a real way with people, whereas me, well my mouth would get me in trouble.'

'But you manage to smile and be polite on reception all day long. Mr Price speaks very highly of you.'

She suspected pervy old Fusty Pants spoke highly of her for reasons that didn't include her exceptional people skills but she wouldn't bring that up. 'Ah, but that's different. I can go home at five o'clock and switch off. Besides any arsey clients aren't really my problem; somebody else has to deal with them because it's not usually me they're arsey with. No, Aisling's got the patience of a saint when it comes to our guests. *The customer's always right,* she says, whereas I'd be after telling them they had a face on them that would draw rats from a barn.'

Michael laughed. 'Well, you can't have that I suppose.'

'No.'

They lapsed into a brief silence.

'Tell me more. I like listening to you. You've a magical way of talking, Moira.'

'What do you mean?'

'I mean every sentence is a story. You're like one of the talking books you can get out of the library. I could listen to you for hours.'

'Ah, Jaysus, is that polite of way saying I've been talking about myself non-stop for the last hour?'

'Not at all. I mean it.'

'No fair's fair, enough about me, it's your turn.' Her stomach tightened as she broached the elephant in the room. His eyes followed her gaze to his left hand.

'Well, I'm married but I think you probably guessed that?'

She nodded, busying herself with her pint glass, drinking too quickly from it.

'My wife's background is in law too, although she hasn't practised since we had the girls. We met at university and got married shortly after we graduated. It's an old story, but it happens to be true, we were too young when we got married, we had our children and grew up together. Then, somewhere along the way for no particular reason, we fell out of love.'

'Then why are you still with her?' Moira blurted out, the drink making her bold.

'We've two girls, Jasmine is fifteen and Ruby's just had her thirteenth birthday.' His face softened as he said his daughters' names. 'That's why. Once they're finished school, we've agreed we'll call it quits and go our separate ways.'

Given her own parents loving marriage, Moira couldn't understand staying in a loveless one, even for the sake of children. 'Isn't the atmosphere you know—' she didn't want to say toxic, but it was the word that sprang to mind.

'We don't hate each other, Moira. We get along well, we're great friends in fact. The way you are when you've known someone nearly half your life. It's just that we don't love each other the way a husband and wife should anymore.' He shrugged, 'I guess it's hard to understand why we're staying together if you haven't come from a broken home yourself. My parents divorced when I was a teenager and it was hard, all that toing and froing. I always felt like I was playing favourites if I asked to stay longer than the agreed arrangement with my dad like I was being disloyal to Mum. I wanted to spend my time with my dad though, I was a teenage lad after all but the wounded look on my mother's face, made me feel like a shit. I don't want that for my girls. It's not their fault the way things have worked out between me and their mother and they deserve a solid foundation to come home to each day.'

Moira was chastened.

'Sorry, I didn't mean to go on but I want to be honest with you.'

She was unsure why that mattered to him unless he wanted to take things further between them.

'Another drink?' he asked brusquely seeing Moira's empty glass. She wasn't fooled by his tone though. Moira could see the loneliness in his eyes tucked away behind the bravado.

'I'd like that, thank you, but I don't think I could fit in a Guinness, could I have a dry white wine instead?' There was something unspoken in his question and her response; an acquiescence that by accepting another drink after what he'd told her, she was accepting his situation. He looked at her for a long moment before giving her a smile she couldn't read as he got up to get her drink.

Chapter 12

Moira watched as Michael navigated his way around the tables to the bar and decided to use the opportunity to visit the Ladies. The cubicles were all empty and ducking into the first in line she set about performing the balancing act instilled in her by Mammy, *Don't sit on the seat you can catch all sorts. Hover, Moira, like a helicopter.* The mantra always ran through her head when she used a public convenience. She flushed and exited the toilet, finishing her ablutions before inspecting her face in the mirror. Thankfully, there was no telltale shimmer around her mouth left behind by the Boxty but she could do with a touch-up. She dipped inside her bag and found her lip gloss, smearing it on before retrieving her phone.

'Andrea, it's me,' she whispered, not really knowing why she was whispering.

'Moira, I'm watching Emmerdale and I can hardly hear you. You sound like one of those obscene callers.'

'Sorry,' she spoke up a notch. 'But this is breaking news. Guess where I am?'

'Have you been drinking?'

'One or two pints of Guiness, maybe.'

'But it's Tuesday.'

'I know that, but guess where I am?'

'I don't want to. I want to watch Emmerdale.'

Moira ignored her. 'I'm at The Iron Bridge with...'

'Jaysus, spit it out would you.'

'Michael Daniels.'

There was a squeal and Moira held the phone away from her ear satisfied with her friend's reaction.

'How the feck did that happen?' Andrea asked a second later.

Moira filled her in. 'I've got to go. I'll see you tomorrow, alright?'

'Alright, but, Moira,' Andrea said before hanging up, 'be careful.'

~

'How long have you worked at Mason Price?' Michael asked, once Moira had sat back down at their table. They were back on conversationally neutral territory once more.

'A couple of years.' She tucked her hair behind her ears. 'I like it, the days fly by and they're a good firm to work for. When I left school, I started work for a smaller firm. My parents' solicitors, actually, which is how I got the job.'

'And you enjoy what you do?'

'Well, it's probably not challenging in the way your position is, although it can be.' She thought back to earlier in the day. The phone had been bleeping with incoming calls, a courier was tapping his foot as he stood, motorcycle helmet in hand, waiting for her to sign for a parcel. A po-faced woman in a business suit who looked like she needed a good meal was crossing and uncrossing her legs as she gestured to the clock and said, 'My appointment was for three o'clock, not ten past. We're all busy you know.' Why Gilly had picked that moment to swan off to the loo was beyond her and she'd felt like screaming, *Leave me alone the lot of you!* She hadn't of course, she'd taken a deep breath and dealt with the courier, the client, and the calls in a calm and efficient manner, as was her job. 'Did you always want to be a lawyer?'

'No, I wanted to be a commercial airline pilot but my father was a lawyer and I told you how much I looked up to him, so I decided to follow in his footsteps.'

'A commercial pilot? Wow.'

'Yup, Aviation Finance was the next best thing.' His grin was rueful. 'I did get my private plane licence a few years back. I belonged to a club in London and took a single engine Cessna 172 up whenever I got the chance.'

'Well, that's impressive. I've only ever been on Ryan Air.'

Michael laughed. 'It's quite different being in a four-seater like the Cessna, you're much more in tune with the plane. It's hard to explain, but you feel connected to it, I guess. You're missing out if you've never been up in a small plane. I've joined a local club here, I'll take you up sometime if you like.'

They were treading dangerous water, was he asking her on a date? Whatever his invitation was, Moira found herself breathing, 'Oh, I'd love that.'

'And what about you? What did you dream of being?'

'I wanted to be a famous artist. I was good at art, too. I won quite a prestigious competition when I was a kid with one of my paintings but I wasn't good at school. I didn't take instruction very well.'

He smiled and she grinned back at him.

'I couldn't wait to leave. I wanted money in my pockets so I could go out and about with my friends, to parties and on holidays, that sort of thing. So, much to my mammy and dad's disappointment, I announced I wouldn't be going on to any fancy art colleges, I was leaving school.'

'Do you regret it?'

'No, I would have messed about if I had gone, my heart wasn't in learning and I suspect that if I tried to make a living out of something I loved doing, like painting, then it would become a chore instead of my passion.'

'I can understand that.'

'I might go to college one day. I don't know, maybe I'll look into doing a night school course or something.' Moira shrugged.

The conversation was easy between them and Moira wasn't aware of time ticking on until Michael glanced at his watch. 'I don't want to leave but it's getting kind of late for a school night.'

Moira felt a flash of disappointment. She didn't want to go home, she didn't want this evening to end but she finished her drink and pushed her chair back. Michael helped her back into her coat and she followed his lead, calling out a goodnight to the bartender on their way out.

It was like stepping into a freezer she thought, bracing herself as they exited the pub. They found themselves on the deserted cobbles with the wind whistling past carrying a light misting of rain with it. The icy blast had a sobering effect and Moira felt her flushed cheeks cool.

'Come on,' Michael offered up his arm, 'We'll find a taxi.'

'There's a rank on the main road,' Moira said, plumes of white dispersing on the wind as she linked her arm through his. She was acutely aware there was no one else around as they made their way down the narrow street ,with its misty yellowish lighting of yesteryear, toward the brighter lights ahead.

'Tell me more about what it's like to fly a plane,' she said, and he did. She loved the passion she could hear in his voice and felt like she was soaring in the skies next to him as he described the sensation of being at one with the elements.

She came back to earth with a jolt as the taxi rank came into view. There was no queue waiting tonight and they walked up to the first in line. Michael, ever the gentleman, opened the back door for her and she clambered in, he shut the door and took the front seat. The driver indicated and cruised off once they'd told him where they were headed. The guesthouse wasn't far and she listened as Michael and the driver engaged in polite banter as to how each other's evening had been.

'That's me just there,' she said, as he pulled over outside the old Georgian manor house. Nina, the Spanish girl who manned the front desk from four pm when Bronagh knocked off would have gone home by now, and Moira would have to use the code to get in. She made a token gesture of rummaging inside her purse knowing there was nothing in there other than a few coins.

'I've got this, Moira,' Michael said over his shoulder before climbing out and opening her door for her. She tried to be graceful clambering out, no easy task, and once she'd alighted, she stood under the street light wondering if he would kiss her goodnight. She wanted him to but at the same time she was frightened. If he did and she kissed him back, then she would very definitely be crossing into unchartered waters.

He pointed across the darkened street, gesturing to O'Mara's. 'This is you?'

She nodded.

'Wow, that's some building.' Even against the street lights, O'Mara's Georgian grandeur was obvious. Moira was used to it, she saw it every day and it was home, but now and then she saw it through someone else's eyes.

'Yes, it is.'

He reached out and stroked her cheek, his touch warm on her cool skin. Then, he leaned down and kissed her on the tip of her nose.

'Goodnight, Minnie Mouse, I've had a lovely evening.'

'Me too.'

They smiled at each other until the taxi's radio rattling into life jarred them into action. Michael climbed back inside and the taxi idled on the street outside until Moira had punched in the code and entered the dimly lit reception area, locking the door behind her.

Chapter 13

That kiss...

Moira wasn't used to dining in places like this. She was more often than not found shovelling a bag of chips down as she weaved her way home after a night on the lash. She wasn't a complete heathen though; she did up the ante from time to time, but on those occasions, Mammy was usually paying, or, she and Andrea were splitting the bill at Quinn's. Actually, now that she thought about it, she really must hit Quinn up about a family dining discount. It was only fair given the amount of headboard wall-banging she'd had to put up with of late.

The snowy expanse of crisply cornered cloth stretched between her and Michael, and she resisted the urge to run her hand over it. The cutlery was laid out in order of service and gleamed under the ambient lighting. Moira was certain if she picked up the spoon and held it aloft, she'd see her face reflected back at her. She left her spoon alone and picked up her wine glass instead. The waiter, Louis, who looked more like a Seamus or Padraig given his shock of red hair and stodgy middle—weren't French men supposed to be dark and lean?—had polished the glasses until they sparkled like an advert for dishwasher tablets, before pouring the wine. A mean little pour it was too she thought, eyeing the contents before taking a sip of the ruby liquid.

It was too dry for her taste but Michael had ordered it and therefore it really didn't matter that it tasted a little shitey.

'Do you like it?' he asked her, setting his glass down, and she liked the way his eyes sought her approval.

'It's gorgeous,' she beamed, pushing her hair back over her shoulder. He smiled back at her.

'I took a punt booking us a table here. I don't know my way around the Dublin restaurant scene but it got a good review in the paper.'

Moira's eyes darted about the room. It breathed with an understated elegance. It was the sort of place that made you feel you were somewhere special; that you were *someone* special. She liked that feeling, her daddy had always made her feel like that. Ooh and speaking of which, she was certain that was the model, Geena, and what's-his-face from that band sitting in the farthest corner of the room. Moira pinched herself under the table—wait until she told Andrea about this!

Louis glided silently up to their table, which was impressive given his girth, and handed them a menu each before spouting off about the fish of the day and gliding away again. Moira watched him go, wondering if he had some sort of special shoes on as she opened her menu and stared at it. It was in French she realised scouring the list. French! They were in Dublin not Paris for feck's sake. She squinted as though that might help her make sense of the words but they were gobbledygook to her. She didn't want to appear a total eejit but if she didn't own up to the fact she couldn't make head nor tail of what was on offer, then she was likely to wind up with frogs' legs or snails on her plate. She wished she'd paid attention in French class now.

'Do you want some help?'

Moira looked up and saw Michael had a twinkle in his eye as he watched her across the table.

'Am I that obvious?'

He smiled, 'Let's just say you have a beautifully expressive face.'

All she heard was beautiful. He thought she was beautiful.

'I'm going to have the Dublin Bay prawns to start and the venison loin with cauliflower puree.'

'Mmm, that sounds divine.'

'I can read through the menu with you if you like?'

'Do you speak French then?'

'Enough to get by.'

Jaysus, there was no end to this man's talents. The food was by the by though. She knew no matter how heavenly whatever was presented in front of her was, she wouldn't do it justice. She just wanted to sit here in this gorgeous place and admire Michael.

'I had the worst French teacher. He used to do this thing with his tongue where he made a clicking noise when he'd finished speaking. It was awfully distracting and it didn't take much to distract me so I used to file my nails under my desk instead of conjugating my verbs.'

Michael laughed and Moira was pleased.

'So I take it that was a yes to me running through the menu with you.'

Moira smiled and nodded.

~

By the time Moira finished scraping up the last of her crème caramel, she was a convert to French fine dining. So much for her earlier sentiment about the food being by the by, she'd managed to savour everything put in front of her *and* ogle Michael at the same time. She'd listened, her taste buds dancing with the flavour combinations she was treating them to, while he told her more about what his younger life had been like. His marriage was a subject that was skirted around as elegantly as the décor surrounding them. Now, she put her spoon down and settled back in her seat to announce, 'Michael, that was the best meal I've ever eaten.'

'I'm glad you enjoyed it.'

'I did, I really did.'

He reached across the table and wiped her top lip with his finger, 'Crème caramel.' He popped his finger in his mouth in a gesture so intimate, Moira felt an electric jolt shock her body. *Jaysus! What was this man doing to her?*

'That's good,' he said, licking his lips and smiling at her, seemingly oblivious to the sensations ricocheting around her body. 'I'm ordering that next time, although I have to say the profiteroles were a close second.'

It was a miracle Moira thought, trying to distract herself from the various X-rated scenarios currently live-streaming through her mind, she'd only managed to get the dessert on her lip. She'd been like a horse with a nosebag spooning the silky custard in. She drained the glass of Moscato that Louis had informed them was a good pairing with the caramel and profiteroles—he was right she thought.

'Coffee? Or maybe a digestif?' Michael raised an eyebrow.

Surely he didn't mean a digestive biscuit? Moira frowned. 'A digestive?'

He grinned, 'As much as I love a cup of tea and a digestive biscuit, to be dunked of course, I don't think they're on the menu here. A digestif is a liqueur or spirit. I might have a nip of Calvados, it's an apple brandy.'

She really was a prize eejit, but he seemed to like her naivety and his manner wasn't in the slightest condescending even if it was very much a Julia Roberts, Richard Gere moment. 'I'll try the Calvados too, please.'

The brandy when it came seemed to glow in the glass and she followed Michael's lead, sipping the spirit instead of knocking it straight back. She could feel the amber liquid's warm burn all the way to her belly. 'Perfect,' she murmured when the contents of the long-stemmed glass were a memory. 'You know, after tonight I think I might have to move to France.'

'Don't do that.'

She looked at him.

'I'd miss you.' He held her gaze for a long moment before looking away and gesturing to Louis that they were ready for the bill.

The bill was discreetly proffered a few moments later in a leather wallet sitting atop a white plate. Michael opened the wallet and without batting an eyelid placed his credit card in it. Moira was pleased Louis was presumptuous enough to have presented the bill to Michael, she had a sneaking suspicion had it been handed to her she would have shrieked, *Jaysus wept!* upon seeing the no-doubt eye-watering sum. She was guessing it was more than her week's wages.

'Thanks, Michael.'

'For what?' He looked surprised.

'For getting dinner.'

'It's me that should be thanking you, Moira, for coming.'

A brief silence hung between them. Moira wasn't sure what she should say to that and was pleased she was saved from doing so by Louis returning with his bank card. Michael waited until the waiter had left them alone once more. 'Listen, I know it's cold out, but do you fancy a stroll to walk off dinner?'

'That sounds a grand idea.'

They got up from the table and made their way to the exit, waiting a few beats for their coats to be returned to them. Michael took her hand, a gesture that made her feel safe and protected, and she followed his lead down the stairs to the street outside.

~

Normal everyday things looked different when you saw them through someone else's eyes Moira thought, gazing down at the shimmering black waters of the Liffey. They'd come to a halt halfway across the Ha'penny Bridge, pausing to look over the rails at the lights reflected in the river. She'd walked over this bridge a trillion times, she knew this city like the back of her hand, but tonight walking its streets with Michael, it had come alive to her with a certain magic. She spied the ghostly white outline of two swans, their posture regal as they floated toward the bridge, and pointed them out to him.

'Moira, I really want to kiss you right now.'

'Oh.' She hadn't expected that but while she processed his words, her body turned toward him of its own accord. She held her breath as he cupped her face in his hands, tilting it toward him. 'By God, you're beautiful, you take my breath away, do you know that?'

She didn't get a chance to reply as his lips settled over the top of hers, commanding a response. The sounds of the city's night life faded and the only thing she was aware of was the feel of his tongue as it sought hers to begin a slow, languid dance. At that moment, she knew she was lost to him.

Chapter 14

Present

The alarm shrilled Moira into wakefulness and she reached over, fumbling around blindly for the button to silence it. The wind had begun to howl in the small hours and the sound of it rattling the old manor house's panes had distracted her from her thoughts of Michael. Now she yawned and rubbed her eyes. They felt gritty and raw as though she'd only been asleep for five minutes. It was going to take a supreme effort to get up this morning. 'You'll feel better after a shower,' she muttered aloud and then, with a groan, hauled herself out of bed before stomping down the hall to the bathroom.

'Feck!' she muttered seeing the door shut and the light shining out from under the crack. Moira had beaten her in there. They'd had this discussion before. Moira needed to be at work by eight thirty. While it was expected that she be seated, headset on, a cheery grin plastered to her face and her hand poised to hit the button for the morning's first call at that time, in order to fulfil her employment obligations and have any hope of her morning panning out smoothly enough for her to have that cheery grin on her face, she needed to be in the shower at seven fifteen on the dot.

Aisling could mosey on downstairs to see what was happening in the guesthouse whenever she fecking liked. Mrs Flaherty and Bronagh always had things under control of a morning and nobody would threaten her with dismissal if she decided to rock up at lunchtime! Moira raised her fist in readiness to hammer on the door, nearly falling into the bathroom as Aisling opened it, an apparition wrapped in a towel and shrouded by steam.

'Sorry, Moira, I didn't mean to hold you up but the McPhersons' tour bus is picking them up at seven thirty and I need to be downstairs to check them out.'

It was fair enough. Bronagh their receptionist who was as much a part of the guesthouse furniture as the antiques that littered it, didn't start until eight o'clock, but Moira was still half asleep and as such she didn't give a flying feck about the McPhersons checking out. So, with a scowl at her sister, she pushed past her and shut the door with the heel of her foot.

She used the few seconds it took for the water to heat up to peer in the mirror. A set of puffy eyes stared back at her and she wrinkled her nose in distaste before stepping into the shower. Puffy eyes she did not need, today of all days. At least they'd have gone down by the time Mairead's party rolled around and she could hide the dark circles with concealer.

Aisling had already gone down to reception by the time she'd finished her morning routine. And, after downing one coffee and having shovelled down a bowl of cereal, she felt ready to re-join the human race. The only sound breaking the silence was the tick-tock of the old grandfather clock in the corner of the room; an heirloom passed down on her daddy's side just like O'Mara's itself. She glanced at it to check the time and saw she had ten minutes before she'd need to slide her feet into her runners and head out the door for work. With the congested rush hour streets, it was faster for her to walk to work than to cadge a lift or catch the bus. Ten minutes was plenty of time to give Roisin a call and tell her what Mammy had planned. She'd need to keep the call short anyway, calling rates to the UK this time of the day were ridiculous.

Moira picked up the phone and hit the number saved to speed dial before cradling the phone against her shoulder to walk over to the dining room table to retrieve her cereal bowl. She wasn't in the mood for Aisling giving out about her slovenly ways, so she carried it back into the kitchen, dumping it in the sink. The phone kept ringing. 'Come on, Rosie,' she muttered as the seconds ticked by.

'Hello,' her brother-in-law answered.

She was surprised to hear his harried and self-important voice given he'd normally have left for work by now. 'How're you, Colin? It's Moira. Late start today is it?'

She half expected him to tell her to mind her own business, but he didn't, answering snippily, 'I've been working from home.'

Poor Rosie, Moira thought. 'I see. That's erm, nice. I was after a quick word with Rosie if she's about?'

There was a sigh. 'It's not a great time, she's got to get Noah ready for school. Is it urgent Moira? Or, can I pass on a message?'

He was such a controlling arse, she thought sparking with irritation. 'It is rather urgent, Colin, I won't keep her long.'

Another sigh. 'I'll get her for you.'

Moira pulled a face at the phone and drummed her fingers on the kitchen bench as she waited for her sister. What Rosie had seen in Colin was beyond her. The man had no chin for feck's sake and had earned himself the nickname Colin the Arse within minutes of meeting the family. No chin said a lot about the character of a person in her book. Then again, she thought as Noah's bright painting on the fridge caught her eye, if Rosie hadn't of met Colin there'd be no Noah, and Moira adored her nephew and his perfectly normal chin.

'Moira, what's happened? Colin said you told him it was urgent. Is Mammy alright?'

'Yes and no, Rosie. She's taken leave of her senses, but in the physical sense she's perfectly fine.'

'I don't have time for this, Moira, spit it out. Noah's got to leave for school in ten minutes and he's not being very cooperative. He won't eat his bloody cornflakes.'

She heard Colin in the background admonish his wife for swearing and Moira gave him a two-fingered salute down the phone on her behalf.

'She's only after booking a trip for herself and her friend, yer one who had the hip replacement, to go to Vietnam. She says she wants to sail on a junk.'

'Noah don't do that with your spoon.'

Moira frowned, she wanted her sister's full attention. 'Did you hear what I said, Rosie?'

'Something about Mammy going to Vietnam and having a hip replacement on a junk.'

'Rosie!'

'What?'

'She's not going to Vietnam for a hip replacement. Her hips are fine. It's her friend what's-her-name who had her hips done and she wants to sail on a junk. It's mad. The whole idea of it is bonkers.'

'Noah, eat your fe—,' her voice broke off and Moira heard her take a couple of rapid breaths. She'd probably been taught that in those breathing classes she was so fond of, she mused. Her sister had more money than sense sometimes. Sure breathing was not hard. You inhaled, you exhaled and then you repeated the exercise. 'Noah, eat your cornflakes please, for Mammy,' Roisin said in a much calmer voice.

Moira, however, felt her blood pressure rise. This was hopeless. 'Rosie, did you hear what I said?'

'Yes, and I don't know why you've got your knickers in such a knot. Mammy's a grown up, Moira. She's perfectly entitled to go on holiday.'

'Yes, I agree, but not to Vietnam. Jaysus you know what she's like. She's liable to offer to carry some random drug smuggler's bag through customs, and she'll get busted because what's-her-name will set the sensors off with whatever it was they used to replace her hips with.' Andrea had filled her in on what happened to Bridget Jones in the Edge of Reason. Unlike her sister, Moira hadn't picked up a book in years but Andrea liked to read little excerpts out for her when they were on their lunch break. And, yes, she knew Bridget had been in Thailand at the time but sure the two countries were just around the corner from each other. 'That, or the junk she picks will have a rip in its sail, or she'll get fecking malaria or something.' Moira's breath caught in her throat, the varying scenes were playing out vividly in her head. She'd have a panic attack at this rate.

'What exactly do you want me to do about it, Moira?'

'I want you to talk her out of going. Why can't she be like normal mammies and have a week in the sun? I want her to go somewhere on the continent where she can complain the hygiene's dodgy, and the foreign food's upsetting her tummy.'

'But she can do that in Vietnam and you should know by now, Mammy is a law unto herself,' Roisin snorted. 'The way it works is she tells us what we should be doing with our lives and totally ignores any advice we give her about what she's doing with hers.'

It echoed Aisling's sentiment. 'I know that but *come on,* Rosie, please. You've got to try at least. If she goes, I won't sleep a wink for worrying the whole time, she's away.'

'What does Aisling say?'

'What you just said and it's different for Ash, she's well-travelled, Mammy's not. What if she got sold into slavery or something?'

'Ah, well now, Moira, they'd be asking for their money back once they realised how bossy she is.'

'It's not funny, Rosie. You didn't hear her, the way she was talking about wanting an adventure, it was very unnerving.' Moira had never much liked change, and there'd been far too much of it since their daddy had died.

'Moira O'Mara, you're being ridiculous.' Roisin's tone softened. 'It's not been easy for her, for any of us. This is her way of muddling through. You have to let her spread her wings if that's what she wants. She'll be fine. Now, I've really got to go.'

The conversation had not gone at all how Moira had wanted it to but she wouldn't hang up without hearing Noah's voice. 'Well if you won't ring Mammy and talk some sense into her at least let me talk to Noah. I'll get him eating his cornflakes for you.'

'Good luck.'

A heartbeat later she heard familiar heavy breathing. 'Hello, Noah, its Aunty Moira. How're you doing?'

'I've been better, Aunty Moira. Mummy's trying to make me eat cornflakes and they taste like poos.'

Moira's mouth twitched, he was like an adult trapped in a child's body the way he spoke at times. 'Well, you know yer man who climbs up walls and catches bad guys.'

'Spiderman.'

'Yeah, him. I heard he has cornflakes for breakfast every single day.'

She could almost hear the cogs turning and the mouth twitching turned into a smile.

'No he doesn't, because they taste like poos and milk is made from cows wees.'

'He does actually; it's the corn you see. It helps him climb up the side of buildings and the milk makes his bones strong. And just so you know, cows' milk is not wee-wee.' God, she was good she thought hearing the phone clatter down.

Roisin's voice sounded down the line. 'What did you say to him? He's hoeing into them like it's a bowl of fe— ice cream.'

'Ah, well now, that would be telling, but I will reveal all if you promise to ring Mammy and try to talk some sense into her.'

'That's bribery!'

'Blame Aisling.' Moira thought back to the deal she'd had to agree to in order to secure the Valentino's for tonight.

'Fine.'

A tick or two later, Moira hung up and after a few minutes of frantically trying to locate her runners—they were under the couch where she'd kicked them off when she'd gotten home last night, she picked up her bag and headed out the door.

Chapter 15

Moira's mood was vastly improved since she'd first opened her eyes. She'd pushed all thoughts of her conversation with Roisin and Mammy's impending trip aside because today was the day. Mairead's engagement party was only hours away. Sure it was a whole day at the office away but that equated to hours, nonetheless.

Tonight she would dazzle Michael when her arrival was announced at the Shelbourne's The Saddleroom. The images of herself swathed in all her finery, Aisling's Valentino slingbacks on her feet instead of glass slippers were all very Cinderella like, but then it had always been her favourite fairy tale.

'Morning, Ita, don't you be overdoing it now,' Moira called over as she reached the first-floor landing and paused for a moment. Her tongue was very much in her cheek.

Ita looked up from her phone, the bucket full of cleaning products by her feet. 'What was that?'

'Nothing, I just said you be sure to have a good day.'

Ita shot her a suspicious glance as she took the pass key for Room 3 out of her pocket. She never quite knew whether Moira was being serious or not. 'Sure, same to you.'

Moira carried on down to reception and perched on the side of the front desk as she did most mornings. Bronagh was on the phone taking a booking, telltale biscuit crumbs down her front. She was as much a part of the furniture as the plush cream sofa with its green stripes in the reception area, Moira mused. The three-seater was where guests could relax and read through one of the many brochures advertising everything from the annual Lisdoonvarna Matchmaking Festival through to Quinn's Bistro! Aisling always made sure her fella's brochures were well stocked just as she fastidiously plumped the sofa's cushions each morning before doing the same thing to the identical sofa in the guest lounge.

Moira couldn't see the point in cushions, they got in the way more often than not, and she couldn't be doing with all that plumping.

Bronagh finished the call, 'And how're you today?'

'Grand, Bronagh, or at least I will be when you give us one of those custard creams you're after snaffling.'

'Custard what?' Bronagh feigned innocence.

'A custard cream—ah go on, Bronagh, I need sustenance if I'm to walk all the way to work.'

'Sure, you're a fit young thing so you are, and besides I don't know what you're on about.'

'Don't play the innocent with me. The biscuits you've got hidden in your top drawer there.' Moira pointed to the drawer before thrusting her hand forth for a biscuit. Bronagh needed her hair doing she noticed, spying the zebra streak running through her jet-black hair as the older woman grudgingly opened the drawer,

Moira shook her head. Why their receptionist was one of life's flirts, especially when it came to men young enough to be her son, was a source of consternation to her. The way she used to carry on with Quinn before he and Aisling finally got it together was embarrassing. Aisling thought it was funny but to Moira's mind, Bronagh should be setting her sights on someone closer to her own age. She didn't let her mind dwell on the hypocrisy of that sentiment given the age gap between her and Michael as she helped herself to a biscuit.

'One mind. You and that sister of yours rob me blind, so you do. I've only got crackers for lunch I'll have you know.' Bronagh patted her middle and gave it a despondent look. 'And they'll hardly keep me going through the day. You've no idea what it's like to be peckish all the time, Moira, and never lose so much as a pound.'

Given Bronagh had just been stuffing biscuits in her gob, Moira very much doubted Bronagh had any clue either. As she chomped she remembered Mammy's news.

'I've something to tell you about my mad mammy.'

'Oh, yes?' Bronagh was all ears, she liked to be kept in the know. Moira filled her in on Maureen's plans for backpacking around Vietnam, pleased she wasn't interrupted mid-flow by the phone. She didn't know what she expected when she'd finished talking but Bronagh's wistful expression as she said, 'Good for Maureen, I say. She'll have a grand time so she will. Sure I'd like an adventure.' was not what she'd had in mind.

'Ah now, Bronagh, come on, sure there's enough adventure to be had right here in Dublin so there is.'

'Not when you're battling hot flushes and a burgeoning middle, there's not.' Bronagh put the biscuits back in the drawer closing it with a bang as the phone began to ring. It was time Moira got on her way anyway and saying cheerio she psyched herself up for the blast of cold that would hit her as soon as she opened the door.

She could feel the air heavy with impending rain as she strode along the street. Well, it could rain all it liked this morning she thought, eyeing the bulging dark clouds challengingly. It had better not dare spit so much as a drop after she'd had her hair blow-waved come lunchtime. Her mind swung back to Bronagh as she weaved her way past the dawdlers dragging their heels on the walk to work. Aisling had mentioned she thought lovely Mr Walsh had his eye on Bronagh. He was a proper gentleman from days gone by who lived in Liverpool although he hailed from Dublin. He stayed at O'Mara's for a week every September visiting his sister on an annual pilgrimage home to Dublin. She still lived in the family home and he always maintained he got on perfectly well with his sibling so long as they weren't under the same roof!

It would be nice for Bronagh to meet someone special, someone kind—she deserved as much, Moira thought waiting for the lights to change. For as long as she'd known her which was most of her life, their receptionist had been on her own. She'd gone out with the odd fellow but that had been yonks ago now. She must be lonely with only her ailing mammy, who she looked after for company of an evening.

All thoughts of Bronagh dispersed as she pushed through the glass doors and pressed the button for the elevator. She smiled over at Hilary, a litigation solicitor with bad breath, and hoped she didn't want to strike up a conversation inside the lift. Her work day, she decided, was off to a good start when Hilary was mercifully silent as they rode together to the first floor. Moira called out, 'Have a good day,' to her as she stepped out of the lift onto the well-trodden carpets of Mason Price's reception area and headed toward the front desk. By the time she'd stashed her bag under the desk and got her bum on the seat, the phone had begun to ring.

~

It had been a busy morning and Moira felt herself relax now, well as much as she could given the current angle of her neck as her head arched over the basin. She was enjoying the tingling sensation across her scalp as Holly, Headstart's shampooist, massaged a conditioner into it that made her think of bubble gum. Andrea was positioned over the basin next to hers and she heard her friend give a contented little sigh that made her smile.

It would be hard going back to work after an hour's pampering here at the salon but she had high hopes the afternoon would pass as quickly as the morning had. Lunchtime had rolled around before she knew it and she'd said cheerio to Gilly before skipping down the stairs to the foyer to meet Andrea. They'd headed out the building's big glass doors pleased to escape for the hour and a half break afforded to them both. Sometimes having that long to twiddle your thumbs in the middle of the day was a nuisance but on days like this, it was a boon. The two girls had linked arms and dodged puddles as they chattered excitedly, affirming their plans for the impending evening all the way to the salon.

Holly began rinsing the conditioner out. 'Sing out now if the water's too hot won't you Moira? I don't want to be scalding you.'

'Mmm' The temperature was just right and she was enjoying the sensation of the warm water trickling over her scalp. It felt rather like a rude awakening when Holly told her to sit up a few moments later before briskly towel drying her hair. Andrea's hair was still being rinsed she saw, following Holly's lead over to a spare seat in front of the bank of mirrors.

'There you go, make yourself comfy. Can I get you a tea or a coffee?'

'A coffee would be lovely thanks, Holly. White and one, ta.'

'Madigan's just finishing with a client and she'll be right with you.'

Moira wouldn't let anyone other than Madigan touch her hair—the senior stylist had the magic touch. She watched as Holly scurried off as best she could in a black skirt that was strangling her legs. She wouldn't get any sympathy from Moira, it was the price of fashion she thought before picking up the latest glossy copy of *Hello*.

There was something a little decadent about sitting in the hairdressers flicking through *Hello* to see how the other half lived at lunchtime. She paused and eyeballed a photograph, imagining what it would be like to be called Tabitha or Tamara or something like while swanning about an old castle in a filmy dress for the day. She settled herself into her chair and was about to resume flicking through the pages once more when she spied the woman seated to her left. She looked different given her head was covered in foils but it was definitely her. She lowered the magazine. 'Hello, it's Tessa, isn't it? Fancy meeting you here.' The cliché rolled forth.

Tessa's eyes widened. She couldn't quite believe she'd wound up sitting next to the pretty girl from the guesthouse at the hair salon. What were the odds given how many million people were currently flitting about Dublin?

Tessa's eyes were an unusual shade of brown, almost amber Moira thought, they drew you in. She watched as a shutter went down on them. As much as Aisling was prone to drama-tising things, she got what her sister meant. There was something furtive about this guest of theirs. Unlike Aisling though, Moira was not one for pussyfooting around. 'Are you off somewhere special tonight then?' Tessa's coffee cup still had its chocolate on the side and Moira fought off the urge to swipe it—she'd not had time for lunch. She'd pick up an egg sandwich from O'Brien's to munch on, on her way back to work. Their egg and mayo was the best. Her mouth watered and her tummy rumbled loudly at the thought of it.

'Ah, Jaysus, did you hear that? Sorry, but honestly I'm so hungry I could eat the balls of a low flying pigeon.'

'What did you just say?'

Moira put her hand to her mouth, 'Ooh, sorry, things just pop out of their own accord. It's the Mammy gene, so it is.'

Tessa's mouth twitched. She liked this girl, Maeve, or was it Moira? She had flashing eyes and a naughty grin. 'It doesn't bother me. My dad's favourite saying was, *I'm so hungry I could eat the arse off a nun through a convent gate.* Mum used to tell him off every time he said it but it never stopped him. He'd tell her he was keeping his Irish heritage alive.' She paused for a beat. 'I'm sorry but I don't think I ever got your name.'

Moira snorted, 'It's Moira and I'm with your dad, that's a good one. I'm filing it away for another day.' She rolled on with her conversation. 'I've an engagement party to go to. It's very posh and warrants a shampoo and blow-dry, that's why I'm sat here forfeiting my lunch.' She heard a throat clearing on the other side of her and realising Andrea had sat down next to her she swivelled in her seat and said, 'Tessa, this is my friend, Andrea. We both work at Mason Price Solicitors.' She leaned back so as Andrea could lean forward, explaining to her friend, 'Tessa's one of our guests.'

Andrea peered around her with curious blue eyes, her hair in dark blonde, dripping ringlets that grazed her shoulders. 'How're ya?'

Tessa smiled back. 'Fine thanks.' Both women were eyeing her curiously and she realised she hadn't replied to the earlier question. 'I've a school reunion to go to this evening, that's why I'm sat here looking like a visitor from outer space.'

Both Moira and Andrea giggled and Andrea piped up with, 'I love an Australian accent, I'm a big fan of Home and Away and Neighbours. I also think Danni has a better voice than Kylie and she's very underrated. I mean, sure, we could all swan around in gold hot pants if we were so inclined but it doesn't mean we can hold a tune now does it?'

'I'm from New Zealand actually, well Dublin originally but I've lived in New Zealand since I was a teenager so I couldn't possibly comment on the Minogue sisters.' Tessa bit back the smile, she'd forgotten what the banter was like in Dublin. She felt herself relaxing in the company of these two women.

'Ooh, sorry.' Andrea was dimly aware that New Zealanders didn't like to be mistaken for Australians. She'd learned this from Lisa the New Zealand temp to whom she'd also vented her feelings about the Minogue sisters.

'No problem, and off the record I'd give anything to look like Kylie in a pair of gold hot pants,' Tessa smiled.

'Ah sure, I'm telling you they're not what they're cracked up to be. They'd ride up your arse and the gardai would arrest you for your troubles if you paraded around the city in what equated to gold foil undies, so they would,' Moira said.

'Hmm, you're probably right and I'd get chafing,' Andrea lamented. 'I always do when I wear shorts.'

The three women laughed but then Moira sobered, 'You've a school reunion to be going to you said? What school? Jaysus, I could think of nothing worse.' She shuddered to prove her point. 'Everyone would be trying to out-do one another telling tall tales about how successful they've been since leaving year—at least the lot I was at school with would. That's not what you've come all the way from New Zealand for is it?'

'St Mary's and no! Well, sort of.' It sounded ridiculous hearing someone else say it Tessa realised as she explained herself. 'The reunion's part of why I came back. I think having a specific date to work around finally organised me into booking a holiday in Ireland. It's something I've been thinking about for a good few years now. I was thirteen when I left and I wanted to come back and see the city where I spent my childhood through adult eyes.' Tessa hesitated, should she tell them her real reason for going to the reunion? Would they think her ridiculous? Because she was going in order to do exactly what Moira had just said, only she wouldn't be telling tall tales. She *had* been successful and she wanted to rub Rowan Duffy's nose in it. She was spared from making a decision by the hairdresser, clad in top-to-toe black, sidling alongside Moira. She was wielding a comb and a hairdryer.

'Now then, Moira, what sort of look are you after today?'

Moira glanced down at the magazine still in her lap and jabbed at the picture of Jennifer Aniston grinning up at Brad Pitt. Her hair was long, parted in the middle and hanging straight. 'That should do it, thanks, Madigan.'

Chapter 16

Moira and Andrea stood in front of Moira's dressing-table mirror and struck a pose, hands on hips, heads tossed back. Moira's hair fell down her back in an iron-straight, dark curtain while Andrea's blonde Hollywood waves rippled to her shoulders.

'Will we do?' Andrea giggled over the top of *Livin' La Vida Loca*—Moira having declared a little of Ricky would get them in the party mood shortly after her friend had arrived. She'd shown up an hour earlier with her dress slung over one arm, toting a make-up case the size of a suitcase with her free hand.

'Come on,' Moira had said, dragging Andrea in through the door. 'I've got the champagne on ice.' Champagne was a stretch. She'd picked up the bottle of cheap plonk on her way home but it was cold and bubbly and would do very nicely she thought, cracking it open and turning the sound up. They had the apartment to themselves; as to where Aisling was, Moira didn't know. Quinn's at a guess. Her sister was in her good books given she'd remembered to leave the Valentino's outside Moira's bedroom door before she'd headed out.

'We're fecking gorgeous, so we are. Of course we'll do.' Moira nudged the pile of clean laundry she'd meant to put away earlier over into the corner of her bedroom before picking up her champagne flute. 'Here's to a sweetheart, a bottle, and a friend. The first beautiful, the second full, and the last ever faithful, as my dear Mammy would say. Cheers!' She raised her glass.

'Jaysus, you come out with it, Moira, and honestly your room's a bombsite. I don't know how you manage to always look so well turned out. By rights, you should look like a crumpled wreck, but I love you anyway.' Andrea grinned, stepping over the jacket Moira had worn to work, so as to clink her glass against her friend's. 'You did well getting Aisling to loan you those shoes; they're a knockout with your dress.'

Moira glanced down at the red slingbacks, pleased. They did go well with the cerise sheath dress she'd chosen. She felt good, and she nudged the spaghetti strap back on to her shoulder before having a sip of her sweet fizz.

Andrea perched on the edge of the bed being careful not to crease her dress. It really did suit her Moira thought, eyeing her from where she was still standing in front of the mirror. She'd chosen a ridiculously pricey one-shouldered, black cocktail dress with a side slit but it was worth every single one of the pretty pennies, she decided. Andrea looked well in black, it wasn't a shade that did much for her serving to wash her out, but it highlighted her friend's fair colouring and gave her an old-school glamour.

'I wonder if Connor's going to be there?' Andrea's blue eyes were tinged with anxiety but hopefully wide.

Moira felt a pang, her friend had been hankering after Connor Reid forever but he never seemed to look her way, more fool him in her opinion. He didn't know what he was missing out on. She remembered the brief instructions Niall had tossed over to her as he waited impatiently for the lift.

'Well, he's quite friendly with Mairead's Niall, I heard they play squash together.'

Andrea sat up straight, 'You didn't tell me that.' Her tone was indignant, 'How do you know they play squash?'

Moira shrugged feeling a guilty stab, 'I forgot to mention it, sorry.' Her mind had been too full of Michael to remember to relay this nugget of information her friend had just pounced on. She could already see the cogs turning and knew it would only be a matter of time before Andrea suggested they invest in some whites and take up squash.

'Niall came out of a boardroom meeting that had run late and asked me to ring through and tell mealy-mouthed Melva that he was going to have to postpone his and Connor's squash game.'

Andrea looked wounded. 'And you didn't think to tell me.'

'I'm sorry, it just slipped my mind, I got busy with the phones, you know how mad the front desk can be and—'

'What do you think I'd look like in a pair of white shorts? Do you think the white would make my legs look chubby?' Andrea interrupted, her mind whirring ahead.

'Sure, you'd look grand in them,' Moira soothed, eager to appease her friend.

'Well, look at you two. You look fabulous so you do.' Aisling caused both girls to jump as she peered around the bedroom door. 'The shoes look fab, Moira.'

'Thanks.' Moira was grateful for the distraction now that her heart had returned to its normal rate of beats per minute. 'I didn't hear you come in.'

'I'm not surprised what with yer man Ricky blaring.' Aisling's eyes grazed the cluttered space. She pursed her lips and swallowed down the remarks that sprang to mind regarding the state of the room. She didn't want to be a spoilsport.

'I'll turn it down. You can't hear it downstairs can you?' The O'Mara children had grown up being told if they wanted to jump around then they'd best get outside because it sounded like a herd of wild African elephants stampeding overhead to the poor guests on the floor below.

'No, you're grand. How're things, Andrea? I love your dress.'

Andrea beamed and Moira was pleased to see Connor had, momentarily at least, been forgotten about. 'Fine, Aisling, for someone who's mammy keeps trying to set her up with her friends' sons. Honestly, the last fella she invited to tea had a face that looked like his head was on fire and it had been put out with a shovel.'

Aisling laughed, while Moira downed what was left in her glass. Her stomach was all aflutter. She tuned her sister and friend out as she thought about Michael. She knew he was going to be there having managed to corner Posh Mairead in order to subtly enquire whether the new partner in Aviation and Asset Finance was coming. She couldn't wait to see his expression when he saw her.

The Cinderella scenario she'd been envisaging all day played out in her mind once more and it was only when she saw the blinking red digits of her alarm clock that she realised it was time they got a move on. 'Ash, we've got to go. Come on, Andrea, we'll head downstairs and ask Nina to call us a taxi.' She shrugged into her coat and picked up her clutch. There was a brief moment of panic when Andrea couldn't locate her shoes but they were found under the bed and, doing her coat up as she followed Moira out the door, they called out their good-byes. Moira shut the door of the apartment on her sister who was calling after her that the shoes had better come home in the same condition as they left.

They made their way carefully down the flights of stairs, Moira in the lead clutching the banister.

'You've got your invitation, haven't you?'

'Yes, you?'

'Yes.' They wouldn't be allowed across the threshold of The Saddleroom if they didn't produce them, Moira knew. They alighted into the cheerfully lit reception area where Nina was sitting behind the front desk on the phone. She looked up and mouthed 'Wow' at them both before gesturing she'd be with them in a minute. Moira liked Nina, they were around the same age and she often popped down of an evening to have a chat with her.

She'd listen to Nina tell her stories about what life was like in Spain hearing the homesickness in her voice. She felt sorry for her having to work so far away from her family. Nina had expressive hands when she talked and a rapid-fire way of speaking but she had sad eyes, Moira thought. Mammy and Aisling might drive her demented but she was grateful they were close by so she could lean on them whenever she needed to.

There were no jobs in the small town near Madrid where Nina came from and the family business, a restaurant was be-holden to the tourist season. She'd had trouble finding employment in Madrid too and as such, she'd come to Dublin where there were jobs aplenty. In no time she'd secured two jobs, O'Mara's of an evening and during the day she waitressed. Her long hours meant she could send money home each week.

It had made Moira feel a little mean hearing this. She'd carried on something awful about the injustice of it all when Mammy had announced that now she was working she could start contributing with a weekly board payment.

Nina hung up, 'You two look bello! Tonight is the party, yes? You want me to call you a taxi?'

'Thanks, Nina, yes, please.' The Shelbourne was only five minutes away on foot but neither girl was keen to brave the elements, not after the effort they'd put into getting ready.

~

Andrea and Moira sat silently in the back of the taxi hoping the smoky smell left behind by a previous passenger didn't attach itself to them. Their driver had driven at a snail's pace around the block in an effort to stretch the fare out. He'd muttered on, all the while, about it being a waste of his time. Yes, it was only around the corner Moira thought, mentally telling him to put a cork in it, but her hair had to come first. Still, given his head was a shiny bald dome she wouldn't expect him to understand. The drizzle that had set in since she'd left work would have been the ruin of her sleek locks and she was not subjecting herself to potential frizz, no matter what.

He pulled up outside The Shelbourne, wrenching the handbrake up with more gusto than necessary. Moira retrieved a fistful of notes from her clutch and handed them over the seat telling him to keep the change. She got out the car quick smart not wanting to hear what he had to say when he worked out, she'd tipped him about fifty pence.

He took off a moment later in a blaze of burning rubber. 'Arse,' Moira muttered, following Andrea's gaze as she looked up at the imposing five-storeyed brick facade that took up half a block. A doorman stood to one side of the entrance and a rich glow emanating from inside the lobby beckoned them forward.

'Wait a moment, Andrea.' Panic assailed Moira. 'Have I lipstick on my teeth?' She bared her lips and grimaced.

'No, you're grand. Am I?'

'Good to go.'

'Right then, best foot forward.'

They moved toward the door and Moira nearly tripped over herself when her friend yanked her arm. 'Jaysus, Andrea, what're you doing?'

'I just thought of something. Well, that's not exactly true. I've been thinking about it all day but I didn't want to put a dampener on your mood. I can't not say something though.'

'Spit it out.' Moira was impatient to get inside now they were here.

'What if Michael's wife's with him?'

Chapter 17

'Miss Moira O'Mara of St Stephen's Green, Dublin and Miss Andrea Reilly of Ranelagh, Dublin.' The tall, angular man with the peppermint breath announced the two friends as though they were royalty. A few moments earlier he'd inspected their invitations before relieving them of their coats. His coal coloured hair was slicked back from a face as smooth as a baby's bum and he wore a tuxedo. It had taken Moira a beat or two to put her finger on who he reminded her of but it had come to her. Pee-wee Herman.

She felt like she and Andrea were starlets in an epic black and white Hollywood film as they stood there in the entrance of The Saddleroom. *What was that old film called?* It dangled just out of her reach as she stretched for the name. She knew it had been a book too, a famous one and the film version starred a dark-haired woman with a name not unlike O'Mara, and a genteel blonde. *Gone with the Wind*, she gave a mental cheer. She'd never in her life been announced at a party before but what a way to arrive! She looked out to the sea of approving eyes that had swivelled in their direction and felt a million dollars. There was only one man she was interested in seeing tonight though and her eyes scanned the room seeking Michael's. She wanted to see the admiration reflected in his eyes.

She couldn't spot his blue-eyed gaze amid the crowd of fifteen or so though and felt stabbing disappointment that he'd missed their grand entrance. She'd brushed off Andrea's words as to what she would do if he were here with his wife with a bravado she'd hadn't felt. Her back had stiffened as they'd made their way to the private function room as she made her rebuttal, 'Why would she be? I told you they're married in name only. They lead separate lives except when it is to do with their kids. Mairead's engagement party is nothing to do with his children.'

Andrea hadn't been convinced. 'I don't know—the more I think about it...' She shook her head. 'And, I've got one of my funny feelings, here.' She patted her stomach.

Moira knew her friend liked to think she had a touch of the 'sight' but she was sceptical. 'It's probably wind.'

'It's not. But even if he is alone, I just can't see what you expect him to do. He's hardly going to greet you with a kiss in front of all his colleagues now, is he?'

She knew that, she didn't expect him to. She'd told Andrea all she wanted was for him to acknowledge the friendship between them. Her resolve to prove Andrea wrong strengthened with each step she'd taken through The Shelbourne. Michael would be delighted to see her here. She was the shining light in his life, hadn't he said so after all?

Now, standing there in the entrance, she was distracted from that line of thought by Mairead stepping forth to greet them. Their hostess had a glass of champers firmly grasped in one hand a canapé in the other, and a welcoming horsey grin planted firmly on her face. 'Moira, Andrea so good to see you both, dahlings!'

She'd seen them both a few hours ago at Mason Price but Moira didn't point this out as she joined in with Mairead's enthusiastic air kissing.

'You look gorgeous, Mairead, absolutely stunning, so you do. Your Niall's a lucky man,' Andrea gushed, and Moira nodded enthusiastically. The bride-to-be had scrubbed up well. She'd chosen to wear copper which did look lovely with the auburn highlights in her hair. Her dress was almost 1950s in style with a sweetheart neckline and a full skirt cinched in at the waist. She blended rather well with the décor of The Saddleroom Moira thought, soaking in the opulent golds, browns, and bronzes of the room. As for the diamond on her finger which she was waving about as though she were teaching Girl Guides semaphore, it was enormous! Moira blinked, nearly blinded by its sparkle.

The tables in the room were laid with white cloths in readiness for the meal that would be served later and Moira guessed the coveted gold upholstered booths would be for the happy couple and their nearest and dearest. Clusters of people milled about the room between the tables clutching champagne flutes, and a handful were seated on stools at the bar. Their low buzz of conversation filled the air like bees humming around a hive.

Moira could almost smell the money in the room. The clues lay in the cut of the guests' clothes and the confident stances of the chosen few. There was an air of entitlement and of being at ease with their place in the world. A few of the faces were familiar from work but there were several people she was sure she'd never met before but who looked teasingly familiar. It came to her, she recognized them from the society pages.

Two young women, each dressed in the identical fashion of a chambermaid from the twenties, were passing around interestingly convoluted nibbles on a silver tray along with tall crystal glasses filled with the palest of yellow-orange bubbly liquid. She'd put money on the bubbles on offer tonight being Dom Perignon or Krug. There'd be no cheap plonk served here she thought, willing them her way.

Her mental powers worked and she helped herself to a glass and, well, she wasn't sure what the canapé was exactly but it had a sliver of smoked salmon on top of it. She popped it in her mouth and munched, only half-listening as Mairead filled them in on the plans for her impending nuptials. She heard the words 'castle' and 'designer' and nodded at the appropriate times. Her ears pricked up when she heard *Love Leila's Bridal Planning* mentioned. Mairead and Niall's wedding was a feather in the cap for Aisling's best friend since forever. Their big day was sure to make the papers and be fabulous advertising for her business. She tuned out once more, her eyes straying over to the entrance on the lookout for Michael.

'Will you excuse me?'

'Wha—, I mean pardon?' Moira corrected herself, flushing at being caught out not listening.

Mairead had that look on her face of someone scanning the room for important people to meet and greet. Her eyes settled on her soon-to-be spouse and she nodded. 'Sorry, girls, will you excuse me? I can see Niall signalling me. Time to play the dutiful fiancée and listen to the boring work talk.'

Moira hadn't known it was possible for human beings to bray until that moment. She managed to choke down the urge to giggle. 'Of course, better not keep him waiting.' Andrea's mouth was full of the latest snack being handed out. She squeezed out a chubby-cheeked smile, excusing Mairead as she wound her way over to where Niall was standing next to Fusty Pants Price and his wife Norma. The matronly Norma's grey coif looked as if it would withstand a tornado Moira thought, feeling a pang of sympathy for Mairead. Being from a fabulously rich family didn't excuse you from being bored silly by work talk or receiving the lowdown on Norma Price's housekeeper's slovenly habits. She'd been there, heard that, at the works Christmas party last year when Norma had cornered her in the Ladies.

It was only when she was safely out of earshot though that she turned to Andrea and muttered, 'Who'd have believed Fusty Pants had a blue suit identical to his brown one. The blue one must be his party suit.'

Andrea sniggered but then as she saw whose head was visible behind Fusty Pants and Niall her sharp intake of breath was audible. Moira was glad she'd swallowed what she'd been chomping on or she'd have been in danger of choking. 'He's here.' She fanned herself as though having a hot flush. 'You were right.'

'Who?' Moira cast about, Michael hadn't arrived yet, she'd hardly taken her eyes off the door since they got here.

'Connor, of course. Oh, Moira, feck it, look he's talking to some brunette. I don't recognise her. Do you?' Andrea squinted over, her gaze intense.

Moira shook her head not wanting to state the obvious. Andrea did it for her. 'She's fecking gorgeous, too.'

'Ah well, that won't stop you from catching his eye. Sure you look just as gorgeous.'

'I don't see how I'm going to catch his eye when he's just about got his nose buried in yer woman's cleavage.' Her friend's lower lip trembled but Moira was having none of it. 'Come on, get that champers down you and I'll get us another. We're here to have fun and you standing around with a face like a smacked arse is not going to win Connor over. You need to dazzle him with your wit. Go on over and introduce yourself. I bet yer one over there can hardly string a sentence together.'

'You think?'

'I know.' Moira affirmed, even though she hadn't a clue.

Andrea took a gulp of her drink and gave a little hiccup, 'Alright, wish me luck.'

'You don't need it.'

Andrea made a beeline for Connor and his lady friend and Moira wondered whether she should hunt down the canapés. She was starving. She'd not had time for the egg sandwich after her hair appointment and, she realised, her hand resting absentmindedly on her stomach, the last thing she'd eaten was the custard cream she'd managed to separate Bronagh from before she'd left for work. She was about to beckon the girl with the tray, refilled with what looked like a trumped-up version of vol-au-vents over when she felt a tap on her arm.

'You're looking even more gorgeous than usual tonight, Moira,' Liam Shaugnessy grinned wolfishly down at her.

She resisted the urge to tell him to feck off and pick on someone else. There was a time, not so long ago, that Moira would have embarked on some outrageous flirting with Liam. The smoothly handsome Asset Management Partner was a popular favourite amongst the female employees at Mason Price and indeed was slowly working his way through them.

She'd fancied the pants off him herself until she'd laid eyes on Michael. Looking at him standing cockily next to her now, she thought he looked like an immature boy trussed up in a suit, by comparison. Still and all, she'd been raised with good manners which she managed to observe at least fifty per cent of the time, and as such she'd refrain from using bad language, for the time being at least.

'How're you, Liam?'

'All the better for seeing you.'

'Oh, for feck's sake.' It popped out of her mouth unbidden and she glanced around hoping she hadn't been overheard. Nobody seemed to be affronted by her outburst other than Liam.

'What?'

'You know what, Liam Shaugnessy. Honestly, that line's cheesier than a slice of cheddar.'

He managed a sheepish grin. 'Fair play to you but it usually works.'

'Not with me. I don't like cheese.'

'Ah, come on now, be nice. Sure, you can't blame a lad for trying.'

'I'll forgive you if you get yer woman with the canapé thing-a-me-bobs to come my way.'

'Actually, now that you mention it, she's a bit of a looker.'

She batted him on the arm and sent him on his way, and he passed by Andrea whose chin was just about scraping the floor as she made her way back to Moira.

'It didn't go well then?' Moira asked when her friend reached her a moment later.

'No, it did not. She's a fecking accountant. So, much for her not being able to string a sentence together.'

'I'll bet she's boring as anything and all she talks about is money.'

'They were discussing inequality and globalisation, actually,' Andrea said, fixing her with a look that told her she wasn't helping.

At that moment Pee-wee made an appearance in the doorway once more and Moira froze. 'Mr Michael and Mrs Adelaide Daniels of Sandy Cove, Dublin.'

She stared at the handsome couple, registering but not understanding that they were holding hands and smiling with that ease belonging to couples who've been married a long time. She felt her stomach fold over on itself as Michael's eyes met hers, his unwavering glance betraying nothing before it flicked away. She watched as his wife, a pretty, pixie-like woman with short black hair and enormous brown eyes, arched her neck up to whisper something in his ear, her hand resting proprietorially on his arm. He laughed delightedly at whatever it was she'd said and she planted a kiss on his cheek leaving her mark before he led her down the stairs. Moira couldn't look away. She felt like a child with her nose stuck to the sweet shop window, watching as they were warmly enveloped in Niall and Mairead's group as though they were all old friends. Her head began to spin and the last thing she heard was Andrea's voice as she said, 'What sort of name is Adelaide?'

Chapter 18

Tessa sat in the tub chair in front of the Georgian sash window. The thick drapes were drawn tightly against the darkness of the courtyard outside. It was where she'd overheard the ruckus of the fox getting into the bin the night before. She'd have liked to have caught a glimpse of him. There were no foxes in New Zealand, so if she heard the clatter of the bin lid again, she'd be sure to take a peek. For now though, all was quiet and she inspected her nails. Ten perfect shiny coral nails to match the bold, coral wrap-dress she was wearing.

Some might think coral was a colour that should be worn only in summer but Tessa disagreed. She thought colour was something that should be used to brighten the dull winter days and nights.

The Grafton Street fashion stores she'd meandered around this morning had been filled with sombre winter tones. What she was looking for was a statement dress and the wardrobe staples she'd seen in browns, greys, and blacks wouldn't do at all. The lack of colour hadn't deterred her from giving her credit card a good workout, though! A girl needed her wardrobe basics and she'd enjoyed checking out the latest styles. Dublin was a season ahead of New Zealand and it was nice to have a heads-up on what styles would be in fashion come winter time back home. She glanced at the bulging carrier bags she'd left inside the door and hoped she hadn't exceeded her luggage allowance.

Grafton Street had also brought back memories of shopping with her mother and she'd walked quickly past the children's wear department in Brown Thomas lest she catch sight of that unhappy child she'd once been. She'd dreaded their seasonal visits to the department store, wanting nothing more than to get the excursion over and done with so they could go and have tea and cake at Bewley's.

'You'd look well in this, Tessa,' her mother would say, holding a dress that had caught her eye up for inspection. Tessa would scowl and snatch it from her knowing that as she stomped off to the fitting room, her mother would be mouthing at the assistant, 'Girls can be very difficult, and she's at that age.' The assistant would give her an understanding smile.

Looking back, she'd been a nightmare but her mother had grinned and borne it. What she never understood because Tessa never told her was it didn't matter what she tried on—all she saw when she looked in the mirror was Ten Tonne Tessie. She should have said something, spoken out and explained why she was being so unpleasant. It wasn't that she was being intentionally difficult. It was because she was hurting. The truth of the matter though was she'd been too ashamed to breathe a word of what was happening every day on the walk home from school. So, she'd stayed quiet, unable to shake the sound of Rowan's nasally taunting every time she looked in the mirror.

Ten Tonne Tessie had been banished, at least on the surface, by the time they emigrated to New Zealand. Tessa's finicky appetite prior to the move had been put down to anxiety over the impending upheaval and as such her mother hadn't pushed her too hard to clear her plate. She knew her parents had pinned their hopes on her coming right once she'd settled into her new life. Indeed, six months later they were patting themselves on the back and putting their daughter's happier demeanour down to the outdoor Kiwi lifestyle. New Zealand agreed with them all. It had been the right move for the Delaney family they'd say, toasting one another as they waited for the sausages to need turning on the barbecue.

Tessa blinked the memories away returning her attention to her coral dress. It had beckoned her over like a beacon and she'd known she was going to buy it the moment she plucked it from the rack.

Coral was a colour, to Tessa's mind, that shouted the wearer's confidence in themselves and to the world. It was not a shade a timid girl wanting to blend into the shadows would choose to wear. It also happened to do wonders for her. She'd stood in the fitting room admiring the way the punchy hue brought out the natural peach tones of her skin and managed to make her brown eyes positively glow. It clung to her in the right places and turning this way and that, she'd known it was exactly right. Now, as she eyed the fabric, she hoped she'd made the right choice. It was awfully bright.

'Stop it, Tessa,' she spoke the words and they sounded loud in the empty room despite its cosiness. The guesthouse had been a good pick. It was central to everything but had a homelier feel to it than a hotel. Outside she knew a steady drizzle had set in, but her room here at O'Mara's was warm and snug. The bed in front of her was made with tightly tucked-in corners and plump pillows.

Tessa always thought there was something special about heading out of a morning leaving behind an unmade bed and wet towels dropped on the bathroom floor, only to come back of an afternoon to find the bed magically made and fresh towels folded on the vanity. She knew there was nothing magical about it whatsoever though. She'd seen the surly looking young woman exit what she assumed was a small staff kitchen to the rear of the reception area the other morning. She was carrying a bucket stuffed full of cleaning paraphernalia and had nearly bumped into her, barely looking up from her phone to apologise.

Her eyes flitted over to her bedside travel alarm clock, the one she could not leave home without. She had no time for the shrill bleeping of most alarm clocks and the first thing she'd done after dropping her bags on arrival was unplug the one on the bedside table. She'd placed it in the drawer, closing it firmly. The time she saw was getting on for six thirty. Saoirse should have well and truly been here now. It had been all arranged. Her friend was to have arrived on the three forty-five afternoon train from Galway. She was going to make her way to O'Mara's and they were going to get ready for the evening ahead together. Tessa had been looking forward to them catching up on one another's lives over a meal at the restaurant Aisling O'Mara had recommended, Quinn's.

Those plans had been scuppered earlier that morning by a phone message. Tessa had returned home from her shopping spree and various beauty appointments filled with a mounting excitement at seeing her old school friend again. 'You've been shopping then,' Bronagh the woman on the front desk had said. 'Sure you're a woman after my own heart. Oh and I've this to pass on to you.' She'd handed Tessa the piece of paper with the time of the call and the neatly written message relaying Saoirse's youngest daughter was running a high temperature and she couldn't leave her. Her face must have given her away because the receptionist asked, 'Is everything alright?'

'Yes it's fine, thank you.' Tessa knew she should have used the phone in the guest lounge and rung Saoirse back straight away to tell her she understood, and that these things happened. She would be going down to Galway anyway to stay with her old friend, it wasn't a big deal. Of course, Saoirse's priorities should lie with her baby and not in revisiting a time in their lives when neither woman had been particularly happy. She didn't ring her friend though. She'd felt a desperate need to get to the privacy of her room because she could feel a telltale burning behind her eyes. She'd been counting on Saoirse. There was strength in numbers and she didn't know if she could face going to the reunion on her own. The thought of it made her feel like that thirteen-year-old girl once more waiting for the bell to ring. Ten Tonne Tessie was always there, lurking beneath the surface, waiting to pull her back into the past.

Sitting in the tub chair eyeing her dress, she took a deep breath and repeated her go-to affirmation for when she felt the self-doubt set in. 'I have a healthy and positive attitude that glows through my smile.' She smiled beatifically feeling more than a little ridiculous but repeating the same sentiment again nevertheless before getting to her feet. She'd come all this way, the other side of the world for heaven's sake, and this was her opportunity to say goodbye to that hated version of herself once and for all.

She allowed herself one final check in the mirror. The caramel highlights she'd had put in at the salon that afternoon really lifted her and she shook her head watching the colours glimmer under the lights. Her make-up had been applied with a practiced hand so it looked like she was wearing a mere hint of colour on her lips instead of the works. As for the dress, well, she thought, smoothing the silky fabric; with its ruching in all the right places, it was perfect. She had no intention of being a wallflower and she looked nothing like that child who'd lived in fear of what Rowan and the others had to say. She *was* nothing like that child anymore and tonight she thought, taking a deep breath, she'd say goodbye to that girl once and for all.

Tessa picked up her purse and walked out the door.

Chapter 19

Tessa stood in the dark looking at the old wrought-iron gates with the neat gold signage: St Mary's School for Girls. The entrance, she could see from where she was standing across the road, was illuminated by street lights and the gates were wide open in anticipation of this evening's party. For a moment she visualised the child she'd been plodding through them of an afternoon. Her stomach would be in knots just like it was now, as Rowan and her crew pushed off from the wall against which they lay in wait.

She looked past that ugly scene, following the expanse of asphalt as black as the Guinness Lake tonight, to the main school building. The gates hinted at a grandness the building itself lacked. It was a bland, two-storey rectangle rather like a cardboard box with windows in it. It was fit for purpose and not much else. The seventies had a lot to answer for when it came to both fashion and architecture, Tessa mused, checking the building out. The spotlights dotted under the eaves lit her old haunt up enough for her to wonder at how much smaller it seemed, shrunken almost from the enormous and overwhelming school of her childhood. It was funny how that happened when you went back to places you'd been familiar with as a child.

She heard car doors slam across the quiet road followed by laughter and stepped further into the shadows. She didn't want whoever it was to see her loitering and think she was some sort of weirdo even if she was behaving like one. Two women passed under the street light a moment later. Their arms were linked and she strained to see if she might recognise them. The light was too dull to make out their features though and she watched them until they'd veered inside the school gates. It was time she went in herself but her legs, she realised, had gone to lead in the seconds since the taxi had deposited her here. She didn't know if she could manoeuvre them across the road and into the school grounds. It seemed an interminable distance to cover. Car lights sliced the night, reminding her she couldn't just stand here like a fool.

'Come on, Tessa. You're the woman who's invested millions of dollars of other people's money without batting an eye. You can face up to a few bullies.' It took all her strength, but she put one leg in front of the other just like she'd done all those years ago making her way home from here. She crossed over the road and walked in through the gates following the drift of music. It was a tune she recognised as an old hit by Tears for Fears—Sowing the Seeds of Love. The song made her smile conjuring up her and Saoirse in her bedroom under a canopy of Duran Duran posters. It hadn't all been bad times. The stereo was turned up as they sang along to it while her mother shouted up the stairs for her to turn it down. She'd always been worried about what the neighbours would think. She was the same even now.

Oh, how she wished Saoirse was here with her now. They'd be laughing at those silly memories together. 'One foot in front of the other, Tessa,' she muttered, rounding the side of the building and seeing the double doors of the gym, open ahead of her. The light pooled out and she was highlighted, there was no going back now. Shouts of laughter startled her as she drew closer. Her stomach rolled over and she breathed in to whisper, 'I have a healthy and confident attitude that glows through my smile.'

'What was that?' A woman's voice from behind her asked.

Tessa jumped, her hand flying to her chest as she spun around.

'Ooh, sorry I didn't mean to give you a fright.' The woman held out her hand and placed it on Tessa's forearm. 'Are you alright?'

She nodded. Her heart was beginning to return to its normal rate. 'Fine, you startled me. That's all.'

She got a glossy red-lipped smile by way of apology, the lips parting to reveal beautifully white, evenly spaced teeth as she peered closely at Tessa.

'Don't tell me, it will come to me.' The woman rested her thumb under her chin and tapped her cheek with her middle and index fingers, frowning.

Tessa stood there while the woman tried to place her. It had taken her a tick to realise who it was that had nearly caused her to wet her pants! Rose Gibson, only the girl she remembered had been shy and mousey with a mouthful of braces. Rowan, ever quick to pounce on points of difference had called her metal mouth, she recalled. She remembered how Rose would slouch low on the wooden chair behind her desk in the hope, Tessa had assumed, it would make her invisible. She'd done the same thing herself. This glamorous creature with her waves of chestnut hair and flashes of red hinting at the dress beneath her coat, however, was anything but shy and mousey! Faces didn't change though not really. They got thinner or rounder and, as the years stretched acquired lines and creases, but they were still fundamentally the same. It had been thirteen years since she'd seen Rose last and she had cheekbones now but essentially, she was still the girl she'd been.

'I've got it.' Rose took a step back looking pleased with herself. 'Tessa Delaney.'

Tessa nodded, 'Hi, Rose. It's been a long time.'

'Gosh, I'll say. You left St Marys when we were twelve didn't you?'

'Thirteen.' Tessa corrected. 'My family emigrated to New Zealand.'

'That's right, I remember now. I was terribly envious of you getting to go somewhere as exotic sounding as New Zealand. I should have picked it by your accent. You don't sound like one of us anymore. Did you move back to Ireland then?'

'No. I'm back for a holiday and I heard this was on—'

'So you decided to swing by,' Rose finished for her, giving her the once over. 'Well, I for one am glad you did and, wow, you look fabulous.' Her smile was warm and genuine and Tessa felt herself begin to relax.

'Thanks, Rose. I said goodbye to Ten Tonne Tessie a long time ago. You're looking gorgeous too.' Tessa noticed the shade of red she'd chosen to wear was even bolder than her own coral dress.

Rose's grin was wry. 'Metal mouth disappeared when I was fifteen. And, for the record, I never thought of you by that name. Rowan, Teresa, and Vicky were bitches. I wish I'd done something to stop them but to be honest, I was terrified of them back then. I've often thought I should have stood up for you though, especially now that I have a daughter of my own. If anybody ever taunted her like they did us, well—.'

Tessa was taken aback, it had been her fight and hers alone or so she'd thought. 'I never stood up for you either.'

They smiled at each other in a silent understanding.

'Are you two going to stand around outside all night or are you coming in to join the party?' a voice called from inside the gym's entrance. There was something familiar about the bossy tone that tickled Tessa's memory.

Rose gave her a conspiratorial wink before linking her arm through Tessa's. 'Come on,' she whispered, 'Lets me and you show those nasty cows in there that we turned out pretty, bloody fabulous despite them.'

Chapter 20

Tessa had the feeling tonight was going to be fun now she'd bumped into Rose. The familiar old tense feeling in her stomach had dispersed as they approached the table in the brightly lit gym's foyer. A woman was seated behind it, obviously the source of the voice that had just called out to them both. On the table was a cash tin, a book like those used in a raffle, and an ice-cream container full of tickets the same as the one Tessa paused to open her purse and retrieve.

She'd downloaded her ticket once she'd registered her interest in attending from St Mary's website after Saoirse had told her about the reunion. Now, she handed it, along with the entry fee—she'd made sure she had the right change for earlier—to the woman. She was familiar enough for Tessa to know their paths had crossed before but she couldn't place her yet. She had an air of authority about her too, even though she looked to be around the same age as her and Rose. It emanated from her and Tessa wondered if she was a schoolteacher.

She was wearing a simple black halterneck dress and her dark hair bobbed sensibly at her chin as she unlocked her cash tin before looking up to give them the once over. Tessa did the same and waited for the ding dong of recognition to toll while Rose rummaged around in her bag next to her. The woman's face was a blank in Tessa's mind as she looked from one to the other and back again, trying to put names to their faces. Rose having located the errant invitation and the tenner she needed to get in, beat her to it. 'Jill Monroe!' she exclaimed, sounding pleased with herself. Her voice was loud enough to be heard over the music emanating from inside the gym.

Ding, ding, ding, went the bells in Tessa's head. *Jill Monroe, of course!* The girl with the serious face sandwiched between dark plaits had always put her hand up to be monitor. Nobody else ever got a look in. She'd been an organising type who liked to be in charge and, from memory, she could also be prone to telling tales. It would seem she'd morphed into a serious-faced woman who'd no doubt put her hand up to be in charge of the door for this reunion fundraiser. In fact, if she was anything like what she'd been like as a child, she'd probably been the one who'd organised the whole event.

'It's Rose Gibson and Tessa Delaney, Jill. Or, you might re-member us as Metal Mouth and Ten Tonne Tessie,' Rose ex-plained, realising Jill hadn't twigged as to who they were.

Jill's jaw dropped as she stared at them both. Tessa took the opportunity to explain herself, unsure if Jill would remem-ber her even having been reminded of that awful nickname. 'I wasn't actually at St Mary's in 1989. I left a few years earlier. My parents and I emigrated to New Zealand in eighty-six when I was thirteen.'

Jill nodded. 'Yes, I remember. We were all terribly envious of you jetting off to the other side of the world.' Her words echoed Rose's.

The grass always seemed greener elsewhere, Tessa mused.

'And, so you know, I reported Rowan and her awful friends to the head sister more than once over the way they treated you both, but they were a law unto themselves.'

'Really?' People had cared, Tessa realised; it came as a shock.

Jill nodded, 'I can't stand bullies.'

Tessa was uncertain what to say, so she reiterated Rose's thank you. 'Are they here then?' 'Rowan and the others?' She felt a wave of nausea as she waited for Jill's reply.

'I don't know. I've only been on the door for twenty minutes, Sherie Milligan was manning the fort while I dealt with a last-minute panic over the sound system. It's all sorted now. I'd be surprised if she is here, I doubt she's got very fond memories of St Mary's. She was expelled after all. Anyway enough about her.' She gave a dismissive wave. 'Have you moved back to Ireland then, because New Zealand's an awful long way to travel for a school reunion?'

Tessa barely heard Jill's questions; her mind was on Rowan. She'd be here, she had to come because she hadn't travelled to the other side of the world for her to be a no show. Besides, she told herself, a reunion was just the sort of thing someone like Rowan would go to. Like the old Bruce Springsteen song, she'd want to relive her glory days when she ruled the roost.

'Tessa?'

'Oh, sorry. No, I haven't moved back to Dublin. I live in Auckland. I'm here on holiday, revisiting my old haunts and I plan on travelling around for a week or so. Saoirse Hagan and I have kept in touch over the years and she knew I was going to be here at the same time as the reunion and wrote to me about it. I thought it would be fun to come along and catch up with some old faces.'

'Well, I'd never have recognised the pair of you! You're both looking very well on it. What is it you're doing with yourselves these days?'

Rose went first and Tessa listened, curious to find out what she was up to. 'I've a four-year-old daughter, Ella, and I work in PR,' she said, and Tessa wasn't surprised. She looked like the sort of self-assured woman who would work in what she'd always perceived to be the glamorous world of public relations. Good for her rising above the slights of her childhood. 'Yourself?' Rose asked.

'I'm a primary school teacher, here at St Mary's believe it or not. I can tell you, ladies, your money is going to a good cause, a new computer for the library, and it's Jill Ferris these days. I'm married to Phil and we have a little girl as well, she's two, called Molly.'

Tessa held back the unladylike snort. *She knew it!* She was a teacher.

'Congratulations. Molly's a lovely name.' Rose carried on, 'I'm raising Ella on my own. Her father was a dead loss and I'm happily single again after giving my last squeeze the flick, he had the most annoying habit of leaving the loo seat up. Spot the woman who's gotten used to living on her own.'

Jill looked unsure whether to laugh or not so she turned her focus back to Tessa.

'I'm an investment consultant. The hours don't leave me much time for dating.'

'You always were top of the class in maths and dating is overrated, anyway,' Rose said.

Jill smiled that smug smile of the happily married before asking, 'Is Saoirse coming?'

'No, she had planned to, but her youngest is poorly. She lives in Galway with her husband, Tom, and their two children. The baby, Tarah, is one, and Luke's two and a half. They keep her busy by all accounts.'

'They would indeed. One of each, lovely,' Jill said, before calling over her shoulder into the room behind her. 'Linda, what are you doing in there? You won't believe who's here!'

If Tessa's memory served her correctly, the room was a cloakroom.

'She only went in to hang up a few coats. The reunion was my idea, we're in desperate need of that computer and I thought it would nice for all us old girls to re-connect. Find out where we're all at in life. Do you remember Linda? Linda Stagg?'

They both nodded, and Tessa thought some things never changed. Linda had always been Jill's second in command—a girl who'd been so skinny she'd seemed to be all angles, always eager to do her friend's bidding. She remembered her shock of black ringlets. They'd sprung madly from her head and had been a source of fascination to Tessa. She'd had to resist the urge to pull one just to watch it ping back into place whenever Linda walked by.

'Sorry, Jill. I was calling home to tell James his dinner was in the oven.' A woman appeared in a dress not dissimilar to Jill's only in navy. There was no mistaking it was Linda. Her hair still sprang madly from her head but these days the ringlets were longer and could be called her crowning glory. She'd grown into her gawky body too, to emerge a pretty, if a little understated—who wore pearls at their age? woman.

Linda's deep brown eyes flicked from one face to the other before she put a hand to her mouth. 'Tessa Delaney and Rose Gibson, well I never. You two look fabulous!'

Rose and Tessa smiled their thanks and returned the compliment. Tessa was about to ask what Linda was doing with herself these days when Jill interrupted. 'Ladies, like I said, Linda's on coats.' It was Jill's way of telling them they couldn't be standing about making small talk, not when they had a job to be getting on with. Tessa's mouth twitched as she did as she was told and shrugged out of her coat, just like people's faces never really changed their core personalities never did either.

'You two aren't going to be stuck here all night, are you?'

'No, doors shut at eight o'clock sharp and then Linda and I shall be helping ourselves to a well-earned glass of punch.'

'Fair play to you,' said Rose, shedding her own coat as she spoke.

Linda scribbled Tessa's name on the stub before ripping off the ticket. 'Don't lose that now will you?'

'I won't.' She tucked it away in her purse and waited for Rose. Her dress was stunning, a statement dress just like her own she thought, seeing it properly now she'd taken her coat off and handed it to Linda. For the first time, she felt a frisson of excitement at what lay beyond the foyer.

Chapter 21

Neneh Cherry was rocking as they walked into the gym. The lights were dimmed, but it wasn't dark, and all signs of equipment of torture, such as the vault Tessa used to have to be helped over, had been hidden away. She was hit by a wave of nostalgia, not necessarily a fond nostalgia but rather the sensation of having passed many hours here. There was a band of women shaking their groove thing in the middle of the floor and her eyes raked over them trying to see if she knew anyone. One or two faces were easily recognisable but neither Rowan nor the other two she concluded, was in their midst.

Around the edges of the designated dance floor, old friends had clustered, paper cups in hand and heads bent as they strained to hear what one another was saying over the music. Balloons and streamers hung from the rafters and a trestle table had been set up in the corner of the room. It was bow-legged thanks to the enormous punch bowl weighing it down. There were paper cups laid out in neat rows next to it and the rest of the cloth was covered with paper bowls filled with crisps. The ticket had mentioned a light supper was being served at the end of the night. Tessa had a strong suspicion it would be the stuff of children's parties, the little red cocktail sausages that always made an appearance alongside a bowl of tomato sauce to dunk them in, and a few savoury sausage rolls.

'Let's get a cup of that punch.' Rose made a beeline for the table and Tessa followed her lead, keeping her eyes peeled for

Rowan. She couldn't spot her as they passed by the huddled, chatting groups. A few heads turned to look their way, checking them out to see if they'd been classroom pals but nobody waved and the faces didn't look familiar to her. Rose did the pouring honours ladling the ruby coloured punch into the paper cups. They carried them over to the side of the dance area, surveying the scene.

'Jaysus,' Rose shouted over the music after a beat. 'All this place needs is a giant glitter ball. It takes me back to some of the awful school dances I went to as a teenager, only there's no spotty lads in sight.' Tessa laughed in agreement, it was all rather tacky.

She blinked as her eyes watered following her first mouthful of the punch. It had a kick to it, she thought. Jill had been very generous with the rum. 'I hope they didn't serve this stuff up at those school dances.'

'Would have given the spotty lads more of a chance if they had,' Rose laughed.

Jokes aside, Tessa thought, she hadn't had any dinner so she'd better watch herself. She'd not been in the mood to go out and grab a bite to eat after Saoirse cancelled, but now feeling the alcohol burn her stomach she wished she had.

Rose raised her cup. 'A few more of these and we'll all be hugging one another like we're long lost family.'

The familiar guitar chords of *Sweet Child o' Mine* began to play and Rose shouted again. 'Oh, I used to love this song, I wanted to marry Axl Rose, he was such a bad boy.'

'I was a Jon Bonjovi girl,' Tessa shouted back, grinning. The grin faded as Rose elbowed her and gestured at the entrance.

'Look who's here.'

She felt herself getting pulled back in time as she saw Rowan saunter in through the doors, her henchmen, Teresa and Vicky flanking her on either side. The trio were an advertisement for satin in blue, green, and pink, each wearing a different style—baby-doll, slip, and tube. The longer Tessa stared at them the more she could see the subtle differences of time. They were all thinner of face, the pubescent plumpness having dispersed, but looked harder around the edges.

Rowan would have been a pretty girl when she was younger if her favourite expression hadn't been a sneer. She was only twenty-six but the years since Tessa had last seen her hadn't been overly kind she decided, finishing her inventory. The blue shimmery fabric of her dress was stretched tight across her middle, the tube style an unflattering mistake. It looked, she cast about for the right word, tawdry, that was it. The sneer she saw had been replaced by a thin mean little line of a mouth. It hinted at a life that wasn't turning out the way she'd thought it would.

Tessa hadn't known what she'd do or say when she saw Rowan. Oh, she'd had plenty of one-sided conversations with her inside her head in the months since she'd booked her ticket back to Ireland. Now she was here though, her mind had gone blank, but her feet seemed to have taken on a life of their own. They began to carry her across the gymnasium floor. She barely registered Rose asking her what she was doing. How could she answer when she didn't have a clue herself?

Rowan was leaning in to Vicky's ear and whatever she was saying was making her laugh, Tessa saw the flash of a silver stud in Vicky's open mouth. It was Teresa who nudged Rowan as Tessa came to a halt in front of them. She could sense Rose behind her, hovering uncertainly, wary perhaps of a scene reminiscent of WWE women's wrestling.

'Hello, ladies. Do you remember me?' She had to shout but her voice was strong and steady as she eyeballed each of them in turn.

Three blank over-made canvases stared back at her. Rowan spoke up and her tone was a little belligerent as she sensed from Tessa's body language this was someone they hadn't been pally with. 'Should we? I don't have a clue who you are, sorry.' She looked to each of her friends to see if they were any the wiser but they were shaking their heads, too.

She was still the ringleader, then, Tessa thought at the same time as she wondered who this confident woman in a coral dress was. This woman wasn't in the least intimidated by the trio. They were like the Three Stooges, and the analogy made her smirk. Looking at them now, she wondered how she'd ever let them have the power to hurt her. Well, never again. She liked this version of herself she decided, before enlightening them. 'It me, Tessa, Tessa Delaney or you'd probably remember me as Ten Tonne Tessie. You lot made my life at St Mary's hell.'

Rowan's gob fell open revealing a piece of gum moulded to her bottom molars.

'Feck, I'd never have recognised you.' She closed her mouth and the muscle in the side of her jaw moved rapidly as she chewed her gum, trying to gather herself. 'Ah, well we're all grownups now. Sure, that stuff was all just a bit of fun.' She waved her hand as though dismissing Tessa.

'Yeah, it was a laugh, that's all. We were kids we didn't mean anything by it,' Teresa added.

Rowan nodded and made to move on as she swivelled her head toward each of her friends. 'C'mon, let's get this party started.'

'Fun?' Tessa squared up in front of them.

Rowan looked uncomfortable and very, very small as her eyes darted toward Vicky and then Teresa making sure they were still there, on side.

'Look, it was dumb kids stuff that's all. Move on.'

'Oh, I have. I've well and truly moved on. But I came here tonight to tell you that you don't matter. None of you matter.' Tessa looked each of them in the eye and as they looked everywhere but at her, she held her gaze steady. 'I turned out pretty darn good despite your best efforts and I just hope if you've got kids or when you do, that they never have to go through what you put me, or Rose here, through.' Then and only then did she step aside and let them scuttle past.

Rose came and stood alongside her, she clapped slowly. 'Well done, you. If I had pom-poms, I'd be waving them about.'

'Thank you. I have to say that felt pretty, bloody amazing and it was long overdue. You know what, Rose? I'm going to go. It was great seeing you again, but I've done what I came here to do.' She gave her old classmate a tight squeeze and then walked out of the gymnasium with her head held high.

Chapter 22

'You should have stayed. It's not fair you missing out on a slap-up meal, because I made an eejit of myself,' Moira muttered, although she was glad her friend was by her side. Andrea had her arm linked firmly through hers as they walked down the darkened pavement toward O'Mara's. 'And these bloody shoes are killing me.' She didn't add that she felt as though she'd been slapped. The shock of seeing Michael with his wife hadn't worn off. She doubted she would ever wipe the image of the intimate exchange she'd witnessed between them from her mind. She felt—what did she feel? Angry? Sad? No, not one, not the other, both. She wanted to cry and she wanted to kick something—not that she'd dare to in Aisling's Valentino's.

'Ah, sure it could have happened to anyone,' Andrea soothed, and not for the first time since they'd left The Shelbourne. 'And you'd do the same thing for me. Besides in case you didn't notice I wasn't exactly having the time of my life. It wasn't my idea of fun watching Connor and the accountant getting up close and personal.'

Oh yes, the beautiful accountant. She'd forgotten about her. Poor Andrea. And she was right, she would do the same for her but she wasn't mollified. 'It didn't happen to anyone though did it? It happened to me.' Moira had felt like Cinderella arriving at the party earlier and she'd behaved exactly like Cinderella in the end too, fleeing the ball. In her version of the fairy tale, however, Prince Charming hadn't come running after her. Oh, no, he'd stayed at the party with his wife. He'd shown her precisely where his loyalties lay. The bastard hadn't even checked to see if she was alright. She could have hit her head or anything when she passed out for all he knew.

She glanced down. At least she had both the Valentino's on her feet, small mercies and all that, because she didn't fancy having to answer to Aisling if she arrived home missing a shoe.

'How're you feeling now? The fresh air's got to be helping.'

'It is. That will teach me to drink on an empty stomach. I'm absolutely starving now.' That was something that could always be counted on. She might be angry and sad but unlike Michael Daniels, her appetite never let her down.

'Me too. Have you plenty in the cupboards at home or will we order a takeaway?'

'Things were grim last time I checked. Aisling's always after sniffing around Quinn's kitchen these days. I think we might have to get a Chinese.' Her mouth watered at the thought of lemon chicken and she marvelled that she could summon up such enthusiasm at the thought of food despite her heart being broken.

'Fine by me.' Andrea squeezed her arm. 'You know, Moira, it could have been worse. I bet Michael was bricking it when he saw you there because you could have made a scene. You could have outed him as the cheating, lying bastard he is, in front of his wife and colleagues. All you did was faint and you even managed to do that gracefully. I didn't see so much as a flash of knickers as you crumpled to the floor.'

'It's not quite all I did, Andrea. I was sick all down the front of my new dress,' Moira reminded her friend, shooting her a look. She was unsure if she was trying to be funny and make light of the situation. It might be something she'd look back on in ten years' time with a giggle and a, *Do you remember that night I made a holy show of myself at The Shelbourne?* And yes, the look of horror on snooty Mrs Price's face should have been caught on camera. Right now though, passing out at Posh Mairead's engagement party in front of the senior partners of the firm she worked for, and—oh Jaysus, the shame of it—throwing up down the front of her dress when she came to, was not in the least bit humorous.

It had all been too much. The pre-loading party fizz getting ready and the classy bubbles at the party with nothing to bounce off except a solitary canapé. Then she'd seen Michael and his wife. The look they'd shared flashed before her and she felt scalded by the memory of it. She'd felt like a voyeur as she gawped over at the entrance where they were standing. It was such an intimate exchange and there'd been nothing about it that suggested they were a couple who were married in name only. If that were the case then they deserved a flipping Oscar. It had dawned on her then that she'd been played and the room had begun to spin in a twirling mass of golds and browns. She'd felt as if she were in the midst of a washing machine's spin cycle as everything faded to black.

She'd felt such a fool coming around to a sea of concerned faces only to hurl the bubbles she'd been quaffing down her front like a silly little girl who couldn't hold her drink. She was a silly little girl. A stupid, naïve cliché. Thank goodness for Andrea. She'd given Mairead and Niall their apologies, blaming a dodgy imaginary egg sandwich she'd had for lunch on her being unwell, before hustling her out the door. Could you even get food poisoning from an egg sandwich? she wondered. As for Michael, feck him. It was his fault she'd been necking the champers in the first place. Alright, he hadn't literally forced it down her throat but the jangling anticipatory nerves she'd felt waiting for him to arrive had been a good incentive. It was an incident she had no wish to take any personal responsibility for whatsoever.

A taxi was pulling up outside O'Mara's as they approached and Moira checked to see her coat was buttoned up. She didn't want any of the guests seeing the mess down the front of her dress. The door of the cab opened and out climbed a woman who she recognised as Tessa Delaney, their Kiwi guest. She heard her thanking the driver before closing the door and taking the few short steps to the guesthouse entrance.

'Isn't that yer woman we met in the hairdressers at lunchtime?' Andrea asked. 'I thought she had a school reunion to go to?'

'She did,' Moira answered non-committally. She'd enjoyed her chat with Tessa at lunchtime but was hoping she wouldn't look their way now. She wasn't in the mood to make small talk with anyone, even if she was a little curious as to why her evening appeared to have been cut short too.

'I liked her, she seemed fun,' said Andrea, and before Moira could stop her, she called out. 'Hello, there!'

Tessa's hand was on the door knob and she dropped it seeing Moira and Andrea making their way toward her. 'Hi,' she smiled at them. 'You're not back from your engagement party already are you?'

She looked different Moira thought on closer inspection, and it wasn't because she was all dolled up. It was something else, her eyes maybe? Whatever it was, she was too hungry to analyse it further.

'We could say the same about you. Your reunion can't have been much of a knees up. It's not even nine o'clock yet.'

'I'd caught up with the people I wanted to see and couldn't see the point in hanging around. Your turn.'

Andrea glanced at Moira who threatened her with a black look. It didn't deter her. She put her hand up to her mouth as though whispering a secret. 'She had a little whoopsie and we had to leave, quick smart.'

Tessa nodded in understanding although she hadn't a clue what a whoopsie was. A drink or food spillage, perhaps? And speaking of food she was ravenous. Suddenly the thought of going back to her empty room to order something in seemed very unappealing. 'Listen if you two haven't eaten yet do you fancy heading out for a bite. You said yourselves it's only nine o'clock.'

'We were going to order a Chinese but sure, look at us, we're all dressed up. It would be a shame not to make the most of it. Though my hair's probably doing a Shirley Temple with this drizzle.' Moira felt like kicking Andrea.

'It looks lovely.'

Andrea flashed Tessa a grateful grin, 'And Moira here would have to get changed obviously.'

She couldn't be arsed arguing and she did not want to be left to her own devices, wallowing in an empty apartment while stuffing her face on Lemon Chicken. 'C'mon then you two, get inside. You can wait for me in reception, I'll only be a tick.'

Tessa opened the door and they bundled in. Nina looked up from her filing.

'Hi, Nina,' Moira said, rubbing her hands at being back in the warmth.

'You're back so early!' Nina shook her head. 'In Spain, the party does not start until at least ten o'clock.'

'We're not stopping. I'm just racing upstairs to change my dress, I had a little spillage.'

'Your beautiful dress, you can—how you say?' she mimed wiping at it.

'Sponge it?'

'Yes, sponge it.'

'I hope so, Nina.' Actually, she thought, she never wanted to see this dress ever again after tonight. She wouldn't be sponging it or, or getting it dry-cleaned, she'd be balling it up and binning it.

Tessa shrugged out of her coat revealing an eye-catching coral dress. 'It's lovely and warm in here,' she said, picking up one of Quinn's brochures from the rack and waving it. 'I'd planned on going here for dinner with my friend Saoirse before the reunion. It sounds great.'

'Quinn's?'

'Mmm.'

'It is but I'm biased. Quinn and my sister are doing the wild thing.' Moira looked up the stairs, 'Hopefully not as we speak.' She'd be sure to knock loudly on the door before entering the apartment. It wasn't likely they'd be there, not with Saturday being the restaurant's busiest night but Aisling had thought she was out for the evening. Jaysus the sight of the pair them swinging naked from the rafters would finish her off. She couldn't be doing with that on an empty tummy.

'She's not biased, Quinn's is well worth a visit,' Andrea said, taking her coat off and sitting down on the sofa to wait while Moira sorted herself out. 'The food's gorgeous and the craic's always great. I say Quinn's it is.'

Tessa looked at Moira who had her hand on the banister. 'What do you think? Does it get your vote too?'

Moira nodded, and as she took to the stairs she called down, 'But if Aisling's there and asks any awkward questions as to why we're not living it up at the Shelbourne, you're both to lie and say it was full of boring old farts.' It was a half-truth at least, she thought.

Chapter 23

The foot-stamping beat of traditional Irish music could be heard and a warm glow was visible through the windows of Quinn's as they approached the bistro. It beckoned the trio in. They'd had no choice but to walk around the block to the restaurant as the wait for a taxi was ridiculous. It wouldn't do them any harm they decided, rugging back up in their coats once more, before setting forth. Moira and Andrea had long since given up on their hair anyway. The persistent misty rain had already done its worst and Tessa couldn't care less what she looked like. She felt very free and easy. A load she'd been carrying around for an awfully long time had been lifted tonight.

'I hope we can get a table,' Tessa said, frowning. They didn't have a reservation after all.

'Oh, don't worry about that, Alasdair will make room for us even if they're fully booked.'

Tessa was reassured by the confident tone as Moira pushed the door open.

Alasdair's greeting as the three women barrelled in the door was effusive. He came out from behind the counter where he'd been scanning the reservation book and made a beeline for Moira. A kiss was planted on both her cheeks before he took a step back, a delicate hand rising to rest on his chest. 'Moira O'Mara, I do declare, be still my beating heart. Two O'Mara women under the same roof.'

Aisling was here then, Moira registered as Alasdair carried on. He was only just warming up. 'What have we done to deserve to be graced by the presence of the two most beautiful girls in Dublin town, tonight?'

He missed his calling, he really should have been on the stage Moira thought, watching as his eyes fluttered briefly shut. He held on to the counter as though fearful he might swoon and then fixed her with a wide-open gaze. 'I'm remembering a time when it was you and I against the world, Moira. I was a poor, struggling writer, you my American bride. We lived in a Paris apartment and survived on nothing but love. I worked on my masterpiece during the day while you kept house. Come the night time we attended intimate soirées with other artistic souls where we partook of intellectual discussions and enjoyed a tipple or two.'

Moira giggled while Andrea jostled her from behind, eager for her turn to hear what she and Alasdair had done in a past life together. It was always the highlight of a visit to Quinn's. Tessa stared goggle-eyed at the maître de who was parodying Hemingway. She was unsure what to make of him. Was he bonkers? By the time he'd clicked his fingers and asked the waiter, Tom, to seat their very special guests at the best table in the house, he'd won her over. Who knew she'd once been Mata Hari and he a handsome Russian pilot?

The three women followed Tom as he deftly ducked around the seated guests to a table in the corner. It was indeed a good spot, Tessa thought. It afforded them a good view of the cosy space which was heaving with happy looking diners chatting over the music. Once they were seated, Tom handed them each a menu before spieling off the specials of the day. They smiled their thanks as he told them he'd check back with them in a few minutes once they'd had a chance to look through the menu.

Tessa opened her menu, she'd check it out in a moment knowing tonight, for the first time in a very long while, she was going to order whatever she wanted. Her days of calorie counting were over. Her days of self-doubt were over. For now though, she looked over the top of the glossy card to the musicians seated on the slightly raised stage area. There was a grisly looking man with a Father Christmas beard playing the accordion, his foot tapping along to the beat. A younger, serious-looking man was perched on a stool next to him. He had enormous owl glasses and was earnestly blowing into his flute. Tessa watched the woman on the fiddle for a few beats, marvelling over the speed with which her bow was skimming over the strings. She'd have loved to have played an instrument, but she didn't have a musical bone in her body. Her eyes took in the rest of their surroundings; the exposed brick wall, roaring fire, and heavy ceiling beams, gave the bistro a rustic and homely feel. She loved it.

'What do you think?' Moira asked.

'Wow. I mean, I love New Zealand. It's home, but when I come somewhere like this—,' she cast around for the right words and Moira jumped in laughing, 'I meant what do you think of the menu. I'm thinking the smoked salmon on soda bread for a starter and I liked the sound of the special of the day, the Beef and Guinness stew for a main.' It was the mashed potatoes it was served with that had swayed her toward it. A big mound of fluffy, buttery, mashed potatoes was the best sort of comfort food.

'Oh, I see.' Tessa laughed. 'This place is pretty cool though. We have a lot of good stuff going on at home, but we don't have this.'

'What? Restaurants?'

Tessa laughed again and Andrea elbowed Moira, 'You're an eejit sometimes.'

'The sense of tradition and history. We're a young country. I get the same shivers that music being played now is giving me when I walk in the door of O'Mara's. There's this sense of lives having been lived, stories having been played out within its walls. We don't have that. Well, not to the same degree, anyway.'

'Tessa, that's just a very romantic way of saying we have a lot of old shite in this country,' Moira laughed. Although as she looked around, seeing Quinn's through Tessa's eyes, she felt a sense of pride. The atmosphere *was* buzzing and the ambience just right. It wasn't down to luck either, she knew how hard Quinn had worked for this bistro. This place was his dream. O'Mara's had been her parents dream and they'd set about modernising the amenities while keeping the charm of a bygone era, and they'd brought the struggling guesthouse into the twenty-first century and turned it into a successful family business. It would be nice to have a dream, a passion she felt strongly about. Something other than Michael. It dawned on her, she didn't have any real interests. She'd loved art, but that was back in her schooldays and it had been so long since she picked up a pad and pencil to do anything other than write down messages at work.

Tessa grinned at her. 'Seriously though, how long has the guesthouse been in your family?'

The history of the house she'd grown up in was a story Moira knew well. 'Oh, it's been part of our family for a long time, ever since it was built back in the Georgian era. It was my grandparents who converted it into a guesthouse. With the building's high maintenance costs, it had to start paying its way, or it was going to go rack and ruin, and it's been a family business ever since.'

'You've lived there your whole life then?'

She nodded.

'It must be lovely to have that connection with a building.'

She supposed she was lucky, even if she didn't feel it at times. It was easy to take the things around you for granted.

She shrugged, 'Its home.' All this talk of home reminded her that Aisling was lurking about the place somewhere. She scanned the tables but couldn't see her sitting at any. She must be out the back in the kitchen distracting Quinn from his work, she surmised. Perhaps she wouldn't spot Moira, Andrea, and Tessa tucked away in their corner table setting. She hoped so, she'd be spared having to embellish the night's events then. She crossed her fingers under the table. Aisling was hawk-eyed when it came to her younger sister's activities. She never managed to get much past her. Sure, look at the way she'd known about her borrowing the Louboutin's? There was no way she was telling her that Michael had fronted up to the party with his wife in tow. She'd be liable to march on over to The Shelbourne to sort him out.

'What's everyone thinking of ordering to drink? Shall we share a bottle of wine?' Andrea looked up from the drinks' menu. She turned to Moira, 'Sorry, you probably don't feel like it after earlier. I didn't think.'

Moira waved the comment away. She wasn't missing out. 'Ah, sure I'm grand, or I will be once I get some food into me. Tessa, are you a red or a white girl?'

They agreed on a bottle of the house red and when Tom appeared a few minutes later, they placed their drink order. Moira followed Tom as he made his way over to the bar. He was a bit of a fine thing. Not in the silver fox way Michael was, mind you, he was too young to qualify for that status.

She wondered what he did with himself when he wasn't working nights at Quinn's. A student maybe? He looked a couple of years younger than her so it would make sense for him to be doing shifts at Quinn's to pay his way through uni. That shirt didn't quite sit right on him she thought, even if he did fill it out nicely. It was just that he looked like he'd be more at ease in a singlet with a surfboard tucked under his arm or, better yet, no singlet and a surfboard under his arm. It was down to the honey colour of his skin, and hair that was a cross between blond and brown knotted back in a ponytail at the nape of his neck. He had a cute bum too she noticed before glancing away. Feck Michael Daniels, Moira thought, feeling a surge of righteous anger. He might have strung her along but there were plenty more fish in the sea.

Chapter 24

'Jaysus, Moira, have you no shame? The poor boy didn't know where to put himself. If you'd given him any more of an eyeful, he would have been inside your bra,' Andrea muttered over the top of her wine glass.

'He's not a boy. He's well and truly over the age of consent.' Moira was unrepentant.

Andrea recognised her mood, she was going to be trouble tonight.

Tessa looked bemused. Moira had laid it on rather thick when their waiter, Tom, had come back with an open bottle of red. She'd made a big show of sampling the small amount he poured in her glass for her approval, before holding her glass out for more. She'd managed to convey, without actually saying so, that she really did want more, and if he was up for more, then so was she. The poor chap had been terribly flustered she thought, her eyes flicking to the stain on the cloth where he'd managed to spill a few drops thanks to his shaking hand.

'I know how you operate, Moira O'Mara, and copping off with him won't make you feel any better about Michael.'

'It might.' Moira took a greedy slurp of her wine. It certainly couldn't make her feel any worse than she did right now. At least the acid burn left in her tummy by the bubbles had dissipated. 'And, I didn't do anything. I just wanted to make sure he poured me a decent glass.' She turned to Tessa, 'I can't be doing with miserly measures.'

That much was obvious Tessa thought, watching her swig the full glass. She'd lost the thread of the conversation and asked, 'Who's Michael?' She watched the two friends exchange a look. 'You can tell me to mind my own business if you want.'

Moira spoke up, 'No, it's fine. We're talking about Michael Daniels. He's the feckiest, fecker to ever walk the planet.'

'Ah, right. He's the whoopsie then?'

'The what?'

Tessa looked to Andrea for assistance. 'You said Moira had had a whoopsie earlier and that's why you left the party early.'

'Oh, well, what I meant was she passed out and then she threw up down the front of her dress when she came round.'

'I see. I think I'd make a get-away too.'

'It was Michael's fault.' Moira defended herself. 'In a round-about way.'

'So, this feckiest, fecker, he's your ex, right?'

Andrea jumped in. 'Kind of.'

Tessa raised a quizzical brow. Now, she really was confused.

'He told me he was falling in love with me, Andrea. I think that makes him my ex.'

'I know, but he wasn't free to tell you that, now was he?'

'Life's not always black and white.' It was a phrase that had been thrown at her by her sister but it was true. There were times when feelings overrode common sense or what was right and what was wrong.

Tessa was at risk of a neck injury so fast was her head swivelling back and forth as she tried to make sense of what the pair of them were talking about.

'He told me the marriage was in name only and they lived under the same roof for the sake of their kids.'

'It didn't look like that tonight.'

Andrea was right and Moira couldn't think of a comeback. She carried on knocking back her wine.

'And,' Andrea continued, 'he wouldn't be the first man to trot that line out. Michael Daniels wants his cake and he wants to eat it too. I told you that.'

'Andrea Reilly, don't you dare tell me I told you so.'

Andrea pursed her lips for a moment, before turning to Tessa, 'I did tell her so.'

Moira glared at her.

Tessa was busy digesting the conversation. Moira, she was piecing together, had been seeing a married man. She wouldn't have thought it of her. She came across as having a toughness about her as though she had street smarts and knew her way about the world. She would've given her more kudos than to fall for a married man and especially not to have swallowed the age-old lines he'd trotted out.

'For the record, I didn't sleep with him, Tessa. It wasn't about the sex for me.' Moira didn't want their new friend thinking badly of her.

Andrea snorted. 'Don't believe a word of it. He's gorgeous, Tessa. I'm talking drop dead. Of course, it was about sex.'

'Alright, yes, he is sexy as hell and I did want to ride him. I'd have ridden him all the way to Belfast and back if the opportunity had arisen but it didn't and obviously after tonight, I'm glad it didn't. It was deeper than the physical stuff though. I liked the way he made me feel about myself—like I was worth cherishing. The only other man that ever made me feel special like that was my daddy.' Her eyes burned and she stared hard at her wine glass, willing the tears away.

Andrea rested a hand on her friend's forearm and Tessa wondered how it was someone as beautiful and seemingly self-assured as Moira could be so insecure. You never could tell what was going on beneath the surface; she of all people knew that. She'd never told anyone how Rowan, Vicky, and Teresa had made her feel. She'd been ashamed at how she'd allowed a stupid, cruel name from her childhood to be imprinted on her psyche. For so many years she'd worn that name like a tattoo she hated but wasn't brave enough to get lasered off. Seeing the three of them tonight had given her a perspective she'd lost by moving to New Zealand. In her mind, they'd loomed large and menacing in the background of her day-to-day life. She'd never had the opportunity to work through her fear and stand up to them. To see them for what they were. A pathetic, small group of girls with little lives, who took pleasure out of belittling others.

Tom interrupted her train of thought as he appeared to take their order. He was like a moth to the flame with Moira. Tessa watched in amusement as he hovered next to her while she ordered her starter and main. How Moira managed to make soda bread sound like an inuendo was truly a thing of wonder she mused, her amusement turning to annoyance that he might forget to ask herself and Andrea what they fancied, so enamoured was he by her order of Beef and Guinness stew. By rights, he should have asked them first because it was obvious what Moira fancied and by the way the young waiter was puffing up like a peacock, it was definitely on the menu. He turned his attention reluctantly away from Moira and her query as to whether the stew was 'hot'? He was too well trained to forget the other guests sitting at the table and with their orders hastily jotted on his pad, he headed off to the kitchen. Hopefully to cool down, Tessa thought.

Once he was out of earshot, she spoke up. 'So, I take it this Michael showed up at the engagement party tonight with his wife and you weren't expecting her to be with him. Is that what happened?'

Moira nodded. 'I went to so much trouble to look my best. I wanted to wow him. I wanted to look like the kind of woman he wanted on his arm when he walked into functions. Stupid, huh?'

Tessa shrugged, 'We've all done our fair share of being stupid when it comes to men, or at least I have.'

'Me, too.' Andrea agreed.

'It's just that I never thought she'd be with him. I know, you tried to warn me, Andrea, but I honestly took him at his word. I thought leading separate lives meant just that. I s'pose I believed what I wanted to believe.'

'What *he* wanted you to believe,' Andrea interjected.

'He didn't know I'd be there and when he saw me, he looked right through me. It was really confronting that's when I lost it.' She rubbed her temples. 'I think I will be cringing at the memory of my performance at Mairead's engagement party for a very long time.'

'We'll stick to our story. It was food poisoning. Sure, it will all be grand,' Andrea soothed. 'Remember he's at fault too, don't put it all on yourself.'

Moira managed a grateful smile, her earlier irritation at her friend dispersing. She'd only been serving up a few home truths because she didn't want her getting hurt. It was a pity she hadn't listened to Andrea in the first place. Now it was too late.

'It probably doesn't feel like it now, Moira,' Andrea continued. 'But I think you've had a lucky escape. Imagine if you'd slept with him? And his wife found out about it. Affairs always have a way of coming to light. You know who'd get their marching orders at work if Adelaide Daniels was to have a quiet word in Fusty Pants Price's ears, don't you? Because I can tell you right now, it wouldn't be her husband.'

'Adelaide?' Tessa piped up.

'I know,' Moira said.

'And imagine if his children had spotted the two of you together. How would that make you feel?'

'Ugly.' She didn't want to be the other woman. It was not a role she'd ever thought she would play. She didn't want to feel the way she did about Michael, but it was all beyond her control. It had been from the moment she'd seen him. So, while Andrea was right, there was nothing she could say that was going to make her feel any better. She did not feel like she'd had a lucky escape. She was in pain. She wished she was a child again so Mammy could kiss the hurt better before sticking a plaster on it and magically making everything alright. The pain she was in was very much an adult one though and she'd immerse herself in it tomorrow. For now, she planned on enjoying her meal and sinking enough red wine to anaesthetise any emotion. And she'd had quite enough of talking about Michael.

Chapter 25

'Hello, there.' Aisling appeared at their table seemingly from thin air. 'I was in the kitchen helping Quinn. Alasdair sent word you were here,' she explained, shooting Moira a quizzical look, 'I thought you had the posh engagement party tonight?'

Andrea leaped in. 'Oh, we did.' She gave a casual wave of her hand. 'It wasn't much craic though. They were all stuffed shirts so we left and when we got back to O'Mara's we bumped into Tessa here.'

Tessa lifted her hand in acknowledgment. 'I'd been to a high school reunion which wasn't up to much either so I left early.'

'Oh, what school?' Aisling was curious, still convinced there was more to this girl than met the eye.

'St Mary's.'

'Ah, I was a St Teresa's girl.'

Tessa smiled and nodded.

'Anyway,' Andrea carried on, 'It was far too early to call it a night and Tessa fancied trying Quinn's.' She shrugged, 'So here we are.'

The story seemed to sit well with enough with Aisling but if Moira thought she'd gotten off scot free she was mistaken. 'I thought this party was a big deal because yer man, Michael was going to be there?'

'I never said that.'

'You didn't have to.'

'Well, he wasn't there if you must know. He's poorly.' She couldn't look her sister in the eye. Moira did not lie and she had just told two of them.

'That's a shame, what with you pulling out all the stops.' She checked out Moira's silky handkerchief top. 'What happened to the gorgeous cerise dress you were going to wear?'

Moira half expected her to look under the table to see if she still had the Valentino's on.

Nobody did the Spanish Inquisition quite like Aisling. 'I feel like I'm on Prime Suspect and you're that Tennyson character. I did wear it for your information, but I dropped a blob of crème fraiche from one of the canapés down the front so I got changed before we came here. Your shoes are back in your wardrobe in case you were wondering.' Moira glared at her sister, not liking all the stories she was making her tell. She had turned into a regular Pinocchio.

Aisling eyed her speculatively for a moment before deciding to let it drop. 'Grand. I'm staying at Quinn's tonight but I'll be back in the morning and don't forget about tomorrow afternoon.'

Moira had no idea what Aisling was on about and her sister reading her expression, rolled her eyes. 'Mammy. She's picking us up at half past twelve. We're going to Powerscourt for afternoon tea remember?' She shook her head exasperatedly.

'Of course, yeah, I hadn't forgotten.' With everything that had happened, she had forgotten. 'Don't *you* forget to tell her she's a mad woman booking this trip of hers to Vietnam.'

Aisling shook her head, her hair dancing under the light like flames. 'I don't fancy an ear bashing over my petit fours thanks very much.'

Tom brought the end to that conversation as he appeared with a starter balanced on the palm of both hands.

'Right, I'll leave you to it. Enjoy your meal.' Aisling smiled at Andrea and Tessa before mouthing, *Don't forget tomorrow* at Moira.

Moira was too busy looking up from under her lashes at Tom to pay her sister any mind. He leaned over her to place her appetiser down and she felt his breath, warm on her neck. 'Could we have another bottle please, Tom?' she simpered, waving the empty red as he deposited Andrea's crispy-skinned chicken wings.

'Sure thing.' He locked eyes with her for a tension-filled beat, only breaking away when Tessa coughed. A deliberate move on her part to get him moving.

Moira managed to hold off tucking in while they waited for Tessa's starter to arrive. 'So,' she said averting her eyes from the slivers of smoked salmon, 'Tell us about the reunion, then.'

'Oh, it's a long story. And don't wait for me,' Tessa said gesturing to their plates.

Moira didn't wait for her to tell her twice and she began to eat as though she'd just completed the forty-hour famine. Despite her mouthful she managed to mumble, 'We're not going anywhere. So talk.'

Tom returned with Tessa's bowl of scampi before taking himself off to the bar to procure another bottle of the house red.

'I used to love scampi when I was a kid. Whenever we ate out, Mum and Dad didn't have to ask what I was having.' Tessa avoided the subject of the reunion as she picked up one of the plump, breaded Dublin Bay prawns and dunked it in the thick, creamy tartare sauce. She popped it in her mouth flapping her hand at how hot it was. It seemed right that she order her childhood favourite given how she'd revisited her past tonight. She saw Tom making his way toward them with the wine and while he refilled their glasses she looked from Moira to Andrea. She didn't know either of them very well but what she did know she liked. Moira had been open and honest with her, so she'd return the favour. She waited until Tom had gone, having been beckoned over to a table near the windows by an older couple, before she began to talk.

'You asked me about the reunion?'

Moira nodded.

'Well, I only went because I wanted to show three women, who made my thirteenth year a complete misery, that I turned out alright, despite them. I hated every moment of my time at St Mary's because of them. Rowan—she was the worst—Teresa, and Vicky used to wait for me by the gates every afternoon. They'd follow me home, throwing stones and calling me names. I lived in terror of them.' She surprised herself with how matter of fact she sounded about it and not wanting her scampi to get cold, she paused to snaffle a prawn. Moira's mouth, she saw with amusement, was agape and she'd yet to wipe away the breadcrumbs stuck to her lips. Andrea meanwhile had frozen with a chicken wing raised halfway to her mouth.

'Ten Tonne Tessie, that was what they called me.' She wondered if they'd think her ridiculous holding onto something like that for so many years. It sounded a ridiculous name when she said it out loud. 'It probably sounds funny now, such a stupidly childish thing to taunt someone with, but I could never laugh it off.'

'No, it doesn't sound funny at all,' Moira said, and seeing Andrea tap her lip picked up the napkin and wiped her mouth.

'I used to get teased something rotten about my nose,' Andrea said.

'What's wrong with your nose?' Tessa eyed it, failing to find any anomalies.

'There's nothing wrong with her nose, it's all in her head,' Moira spoke up.

'Moira, you've no idea, you're stunning. Do you know, Tessa, she once got asked for her autograph, this woman and her daughter thought she was Demi Moore.'

'You do have a look of her about you.'

Moira was non-plussed it didn't mean anything. What she looked like was irrelevant. It didn't stop her from hurting just like everybody else.

'And that's what Tessa's getting at I think, isn't it?' Andrea said. 'Words, when you're young and have one hundred and one insecurities anyway, can be hard to unhear. Especially when they're constantly thrown at you. They get inside your head and when you look in the mirror, they're all you hear and all you see.'

'Exactly,' Tessa said. 'And there is nothing wrong with your nose by the way. It is a perfectly respectable nose.'

'And you're hardly a Ten Tonne Tessie.'

'Not now I'm not. I was chubby when I was younger though, not that I'm excusing them their behaviour. I lost my puppy fat before we emigrated to New Zealand. I left that girl here in Dublin. Or, at least I thought I did. It took me years of self-doubt to realise it was never about the weight, it was about how they'd made me feel about myself. Tonight, fronting up to them, it dawned on me that I don't have to prove anything to anyone. I'm me, big, small, whatever, and I finally think that person is pretty cool. That all sounds very deep doesn't it?'

'A little yes,' Andrea said.

'Well, on a not so deep note. It also felt damned good to rub those three bitches' noses in it tonight.'

They all laughed.

'I'd have liked to have been a fly on the wall for that,' Moira said, and Andrea agreed. 'Did you say anything to them about the way they behaved back then and how it affected you?'

Tessa repeated what she'd said, and Moira and Andrea clapped just as Rose had done earlier.

'Serves them right, nasty cows.'

'You know, seeing them tonight, I couldn't believe that I'd let those three pathetic women with their cheap perfume, shiny dresses, and awful gum-chewing habits, affect me for as long as they have. Well, no more. I shut the door on them once and for all.'

'Good for you.' Moira raised her glass and they clinked.

They all had stuff going on beneath the surface, Moira thought, feeling her throat constrict as she thought of Michael.

Chapter 26

By the time the threesome's mains had been cleared away, they'd put the world to rights. They'd also sunk enough to wine to keep the grape growers in Bordeaux in business for a year. A crowd was bopping to the music, which had gotten decidedly jiggy, in front of the stage area, and Andrea suggested they work their dinner off by joining in. A scraping of chairs later they stood up, before ducking and diving around the tables to join in. Aisling who'd poked her head out the kitchen was watching the dance floor shenanigans with a smile as she clapped along. She gave them a wave and Moira beckoned her over. Her face lit up and she made her way over to join them. 'I can never stand still when these guys really get going,' she grinned.

Tessa looked at her shoes, 'You deserve a medal for being able to dance in those. Prada?'

Aisling nodded, 'Years of practice.'

'They're gorgeous. I have shoe envy,' Tessa shouted back.

The tempo was contagious and they found themselves with their arms draped over one another's shoulders as they kicked their legs up. It wasn't clear whether they were attempting Irish or Greek dancing as they got jostled by other enthusiastic patrons. Whatever it was, it was fun and they were all laughing. Moira kept a watchful eye on Tom. He was working the bar and, after a few songs, she disentangled herself announcing all that jumping up and down had made her need a wee.

She went to the loo and after she'd washed and dried her hands, paused to inspect herself in the mirror. Did being heartbroken make you look different? Her eyes looked a little bloodshot and a tad puffy, but that was probably down to the wine. Her mouth too she saw, the longer she stood there staring at herself, had a downward tilt. It was a funny thing how when you looked at yourself, really looked at yourself, you became almost unrecognisable. Your features broke down into individual segments like a jigsaw puzzle. She pulled her facial muscles up until she was grinning. Her teeth had a purple tinge to them and she ran her tongue over them before rubbing her index finger back and forth in a futile effort.

Bloody red wine. It might have stained her teeth, but it had also made her bold. What was Michael doing now? A knife-like pain twisted in her stomach. Was he home from the party and, buoyed from a successful night's networking, making love to his wife with a passion, Moira had thought was reserved for her? The thought sickened her.

The door opened and she stepped away from the mirror as two women crowded in, giggling. She'd do and, pushing past them, she felt the noise of the humming restaurant wash over her as she re-entered the crowded space. Tom was still at the bar and she honed in on him.

He nearly dropped the bottle he'd just taken from the fridge as he turned and saw Moira draping herself across the bar.

'What time do you finish?' She wasn't going to beat around the bush.

'One. Why're you asking?' A playful glint lit his eyes. Blue like Michael's she noticed but wider, more innocent. She licked her lips. Feck you, Michael, feck you.

'I'll wait until one thirty for you in the foyer of O'Mara's, the guesthouse across the road from St Stephen's Green. Do you know it?'

He nodded, momentarily chastened by the reminder this was his boss's girlfriend's sister but simultaneously not quite believing his luck. Tom had never been one to look a gift horse in the mouth.

'If you're not there by then I'll take it you're not interested.' She moved off, not quite believing she'd just said what she'd said. She'd sounded like a brazen hussy. She was behaving like a brazen hussy but she was spared further analysis as Andrea dragged her back into the throng.

~

It was Tessa who gave up the ghost first, announcing her feet hurt and she was shattered. It was after twelve Moira noted. She looked around and spied Tom, clearing the tables. He caught her eye and gave her a mischievous grin. It told her odds were he was going to take her up on her offer. He was definitely a fine thing, but still, what on earth did she think she was doing? Before she could delve any deeper, she felt Aisling squeeze her arm. 'I'll see you tomorrow.' Aisling turned to the other two. 'Thanks girls, that was great fun.' She gave them both a brief goodnight hug and trotted off to find Quinn.

The trio gathered up their things and made their way over to the entrance to Alasdair. He tallied up the bill and presented it with a flourish. Moira and Andrea peered over Tessa's shoulder and both tried not to gasp. Moira knew her friend would be thinking exactly the same thing she was. The evening would bankrupt them but it had been worth it.

'This is my treat, girls,' Tessa said, placing her bank card on the wallet and handing it back to Alasdair. They protested and made a show of opening their purses but Tessa was adamant. 'I've had a brilliant time. It's my treat.'

'Settled?' Alasdair asked, 'Or will we be having fisticuffs?'

Tessa grinned and nodded, 'No, it's settled.'

'Thank goodness for that.' He set about swiping the card while the two girls thanked her.

He handed the piece of plastic along with the receipt back to her a second later. 'You fabulous females will be wanting a taxi, I assume?'

'Yes, well Andrea will. Tessa and I can walk but we'll wait with her at the rank down the road.'

'No, no, no. I've a friend, he'll drop you all home.' He tapped the side of his nose. 'Let me make a quick phone call. I'm not having you waiting around at a rank or walking home on a night like this.'

True to his word a yellow and green taxi pulled up outside the restaurant ten minutes later. Alasdair herded them out after making them promise to come back and see him soon. He stood on the pavement blowing kisses until the cab had indicated and pulled away.

Chapter 27

Not wanting to leave Andrea to travel alone, they agreed to drop her home first, and as the taxi swung back in the direction of O'Mara's, Moira asked Tessa what her plans were for the rest of her time in Ireland.

'I've ten more days here, so I thought I'd head south. My friend, Saoirse, who lives in Galway, wants me to go and stay with her and her family so that will be my first port of call after I check out tomorrow. Then, I'd like to hire a car and explore. I've never been to Kerry, so that's definitely on the itinerary, and I want to kiss the Blarney Stone, do something properly touristy.'

'You're not really a tourist, though are you? I mean you were born here that makes you Irish.'

'It does, yes, but I fancy being blessed with the gift of the gab, so the Blarney Stone it is.'

'Fair enough. I got carsick all around the Ring of Kerry,' Moira lamented, recalling a rare family holiday from O'Mara's. They'd all been jammed in the back of the rusty old Beemer, Daddy at the wheel. Mammy had been driving him mad in the passenger seat with her habit of pretend braking with her right foot whenever she thought he was teasing the wrong side of the speed limit. The icing on the cake had been her throwing up all over poor Roisin. 'The scenery from what I remember was lovely, though in a wild, rugged sort of way,' she quickly added, not wanting to put a dampener on Tessa's plans.

Alasdair's contact in the cab world, whose name was Big Jes, an anomaly given his small stature behind the wheel, chimed into the conversation. He told them a no-holds-barred tale of a wild night he'd spent in Killarney on the edge of the Ring of Kerry. By the time he pulled up outside O'Mara's both Tessa and Moira were shell-shocked by his candid sharing. Moira insisted on covering the fare, it was only fair with Tessa having picked up the dinner tab and she hastily handed it over, keen for the off.

'Well, that was interesting,' Tessa said as Big Jes drove off and Moira punched in the afterhours code which would let them in.

'I'll say,' Moira said, hearing the click that signalled the door was unlocked. She opened the door and stepped into the reception area. It was lit by a solitary lamp for late guests and the light pooled weakly across the carpet.

Tessa shut the door behind her and instinctively dropped her voice to a whisper that sounded loud to her ears in the night-time silence. 'Well, thanks again for a brilliant night.'

'*Thank you* for suggesting it. Quinn's was a great idea and much better than being left to drown my sorrows in a Chinese takeaway and whatever wine I could lay my hands on.'

Tessa gave her a quick hug. 'Try to forget him, Moira. You deserve better.'

It was easier said than done and she flashed her new friend an unconvinced smile before asking her what time she'd be away in the morning.

'I'll get the eleven twenty-five train from Heuston to Galway, so I'll leave here around ten thirty.'

'Well, I'll make sure I'm up to see you off.' She followed Tessa past the reception desk. Her room was situated around the corner near the top of the stairs leading to the dining room area and Moira waited until she'd let herself in before taking the stairs. She was mindful of every creak echoing around the sleeping house as she made her way up the three flights to their apartment.

The old grandfather clock told her it was a quarter to one when she flicked the lights on in the living room. The detritus from her and Andrea's party for two that had moved from the bedroom through to the living room was littered about the space. She'd deal with that tomorrow, then realising it *was* tomorrow resolved to clear up later in the morning. She headed into the kitchen. Right now she needed an Alka-Seltzer and then she'd better tidy herself up a bit.

Once the fizzy antacid was sorting the contents of her stomach, she made for the bathroom. Her legs, she noted were a little unsteady, she had downed a lot of red, but they were keeping her upright and that was the main thing. The smell of hairspray still lingered on the air as she set about brushing her teeth. She wiped a flannel under her eyes to remove smudges of mascara and lastly picked up her hairbrush, running it through her hair before flicking it back off her shoulders. She'd have to do. She ducked into her bedroom and picked up the pile of clean clothes, chucking them in the wardrobe and shutting the door on them before kicking the other flotsam cluttering her floor under her bed. She didn't want him thinking her a total slob the living room was bad enough. The only thing left to do was to turn the main lounge light out. The softer glow of the lamp was much more flattering and she switched it on before leaving the door ajar and creeping back down the stairs.

She felt like a teenager, sneaking about the place the way she was, only this time there was no Mammy waiting to catch her out. Her hand flew to her chest as a sudden burst of coughing emanating from the room closest to the stairs on the second floor erupted and she waited a couple of counts before carrying on down to reception. There was no glimmer of light peeking out from under Tessa's door and she was hoping she'd gone straight to bed. The amount of food and wine they'd poured down their throats should have been enough to tranquilize even the most hardcore of insomniacs. Speaking of which, she stifled a yawn, trying not to think of her own bed for purposes other than rolling around with Tom, and carried on through to reception. She perched on the edge of the sofa in the soft lamplight glow, to wait.

~

The self-doubt began to creep in as the minutes ticked by and a silent conversation with herself ensued.

'What are you doing, Moira?'

'I'm proving I can ride whoever I like and flipping the birdy at Michael fecking, feckiest, fecker ever Daniels, for lying to me that's what.'

'Do you think it will make you feel better?'

'Did you see the arse on Tom? Of course, it will make me feel better?'

'You ate an awful lot of mashed potatoes and the stew was very rich. Are you sure you're up for all that giddy-upping?'

'I took an Alka-Seltzer remember, sure I'll be grand.'

The conversation came to close as she heard a tap on the window. Ah, Jaysus, he'd come. She stood up and opened the door before he decided to knock on it. She held her finger to her lips indicating he needed to be quiet and he nodded his understanding. His hands were thrust in the pockets of a bomber jacket and his hair now hung shaggy and loose to his shoulders giving him even more of a surfer-boy look. For the briefest of seconds, she imagined telling him she'd changed her mind. She could close the door on him and walk away but the uncertainty on his face stopped her, and she pulled him inside. She pointed upwards and then turned and made her way up the stairs, hearing them creak behind her.

'This is where you live?' Tom whispered once Moira had closed the door to the apartment behind them. 'It's pretty cool.'

'You don't have to whisper now, and yes, it is.' She felt awkward and suddenly very sober. Was she supposed to just launch straight into things and jump his bones or should she offer him a drink? She couldn't see herself lunging at him. The cocky, assertive woman who'd leaned over the bar an hour ago and invited him to her place seemed to have deserted her as sobriety sank in.

'Do you want a drink?'

'No, I'm grand.'

'Here, let me take your jacket.'

He shrugged out of it and handed it to her. He was still wearing his work shirt she saw taking the jacket from him and trying not to ogle his broad shoulders and chest as she draped it over the back of one of the dining chairs.

'Have you worked at Quinn's long then?'

'Four months, nearly five. I'm into my fourth year at med school. Waiting at Quinn's helps pay the bills.'

'You're studying to be a doctor?' She wouldn't have guessed that, you really couldn't judge a book by its cover. She hadn't realised it had been that long since she'd last been to Quinn's either.

'Yeah, it's all I've ever wanted to be since I was eight years old and broke my leg, I fell out the treehouse. I was in awe of somebody being able to put it back together for me again.' He laughed. 'What about you, what do you do?'

Moira felt the familiar pang of envy she always felt when she met someone who knew what they wanted to be. It always seemed to her people with that kind of focus were always sure of who they wanted to be too. 'I'm a receptionist at Mason Price, they're a solicitor's firm,' she shrugged. 'I don't mind it. It wasn't the dream, but then I never really knew what that was anyway and it keeps me in the style I'm accustomed to which is living with my sister in the house I grew up in.'

He grinned, 'You're funny.'

It was a compliment, and one that made Moira feel good.

Tom chewed his bottom lip for a second as though making his mind up about something. She could almost see him deciding it was now or never as he took a step toward her and pulled her to him. 'You're also bloody gorgeous, do you know that?'

She didn't get a chance to return the compliment before his lips settled on hers. Her mouth opened slightly and his tongue found hers. He was a good kisser and closing her eyes she tried to lose herself in the moment. Michael was a good kisser, too. She felt Tom's hardness against her as his hand crept under the hem of her handkerchief top and her skin tingled where his fingers began caressing the bare skin of her back.

A delicious sensation coursed through her core and she pressed herself against him. She'd done that with Michael too, wanting to take things further but knowing the timing was wrong. His fingers fumbled with the catch on her bra and as it pinged free, she felt reality crash down on her. She couldn't do this. She disengaged herself from his embrace and took a step backwards.

He blinked his eyes, heavy-lidded with drowsy arousal as he registered the look on her face. 'Did I do something wrong?'

'No, you didn't. You were doing everything right. It's me. I'm a fecking eejit, behaving like I'm some sort of femme fatale. I shouldn't have invited you back here, I'm sorry.'

He looked like a child who'd been told Christmas had been cancelled.

'It's a long story, but it's not you.' She felt awful leading him on the way she had. 'Truly it's not. It's just I've been seeing someone and well, he let me down badly tonight.'

'So you were planning on using my body for revenge sex? Is that it?'

She tucked her hair behind her ear, feeling her face flush with shame, 'That's pretty much it. I'm sorry, Tom, you seem a nice guy. You don't deserve to be treated like that.'

'Listen, I don't have a problem being used, you are more than welcome to treat me like that.' He was so earnest she had to laugh and he grinned back at her.

'Well, I do.' She picked up his jacket and passed it to him. A signal he should leave. She was suddenly exhausted and all she wanted to do was clamber into bed and sleep. He took the jacket and slid back into it. 'Do you want me to call you a taxi?' It was the least she could do. It wouldn't be fair to turf him out on the street at this hour.

'No, you're grand. I don't live far. I can walk. It might help take my mind off things.' He gave his crotch a mournful glance.

'Tom, I really am sorry.'

'So am I. Listen—feck I don't even know your name. I mean I know your Aisling's sister but that's as far as it goes.'

'Moira.'

'Well listen, Moira, whoever it was that let you down tonight, he's the eejit, not you.'

'Thanks.'

He gave her a rueful smile.

'C'mon then you'd better see me out.'

She led him back down the stairs opening the door to the misty night outside. 'Goodnight, Tom. Thanks for being so understanding.'

'Like I said, he's an eejit.' He gave her a smile tinged with regret before shoving his hands back in his pockets and striding off down the street. Moira watched him for a few seconds before closing the door quietly. All she wanted to do was fall into bed and sleep. She locked the door one last time and crept back upstairs.

~

It was too much effort to wash her face, she'd barely managed to clamber into her pyjamas as it was and pulling back her covers she was all set to dive in when she heard a distant clatter. It was a noise she recognised and she moved to pull back her curtains. She pushed her window up feeling the blast of cold air as she peered down into the inky well of the courtyard. It took a moment for her eyes to adjust but when they did, she could see the shadowy outline of the culprit. It was Foxy Loxy. 'Hello, you. Long time, no see,' she breathed and saw two eyes glowing back at her. She couldn't recall them ever having locked eyes before. He'd always been too intent on his covert mission. 'Remember me?' He flicked his tail and turned away, darting off into the darkness. She didn't know how she'd expected him to, not when she barely remembered who she was herself.

Chapter 28

Moira knocked on Tessa's door. It opened a minute later and Tessa stood there looking fresh and rested for someone who'd seen the wrong side of midnight the night before. On the bed was an open case.

'Good morning, come in. I'm just packing the last of my things.'

Moira did so and flopped down in the tub chair. Tessa looked over, hardly able to believe all that had happened since she'd sat there herself last night, a bundle of insecurities and nerves in a coral dress.

'So, you're off to Galway today then?'

'Yes, I'll be gone a week and a half and then I'm coming back here for a night before I fly to London. From there it's the long haul home.' She grimaced. She wasn't looking forward to that flight, but it was a means to an end. 'And, Moira, you'll never guess what happened at breakfast.'

'What?'

'I was asked out to dinner.'

'Really, who by?'

'His name's Owen. He's from Waterford, but he's been here in Dublin these last few days on business. I saw him the other morning and thought he looked tasty but I wouldn't have done anything about it. He asked me if he could join me this morning so we could compare notes on whether Mrs Flaherty does the best full Irish in the country. Unfortunately, I couldn't find out because she wasn't cooking this morning.'

'No, Mrs Baicu's on of a weekend. She does a fantastic fry-up by the way, not that I'd ever let on to Mrs Flaherty.'

'I can vouch for that. I had the works.' Tessa had succumbed and placed her order with the skinny woman. She'd been dressed in what looked like a national costume for wherever her strong Eastern European accent hailed from and was as intimidating as Mrs Flaherty. Tessa had been sure to compliment her when she'd banged the plate down in front of her. 'He was so easy to chat to, Moira. I told him I planned on visiting Waterford on my travels and he asked me if I'd have dinner with him when I do.'

'Go you,' Moira smiled.

Tessa paused halfway through folding a sweater. 'And how are you feeling today?'

Moira's head had been thumping that morning and she'd sworn off the red wine for the foreseeable future. She wasn't going to say anything to Tessa about Tom either. When she thought about how she'd behaved, she felt a searing flush of embarrassment. 'I'm a bit rough around the edges, but I've felt worse. I'm going to head downstairs for a Mrs Baicu special myself in a moment—her bacon and eggs are a cure for most things.' She sighed. 'I could do without being mammified this afternoon but on the other hand afternoon tea at Powerscourt is always good and it's her treat.' She wasn't looking forward to having to say sorry for going on the other night with regard to Mammy's trip to Vietnam either but she'd manage it for the sake of the fresh, warm scones with strawberry jam and the scrumptious Chantilly and lemon curd they were served with. She was drooling already.

'I mean about Michael.'

'I know you did, I just opted to pretend otherwise.' They grinned at each other and Moira's phone burned a hole in her pocket. She'd switched it off and left it to charge overnight and this morning when she'd staggered bleary-eyed into the kitchen where she'd plugged it in, she'd seen Michael's name flash up. He'd left voice messages and texted her.

'He's left messages for me, but I haven't listened to or read any of them.'

'Good, don't. You know exactly what they'll say. Delete them, Moira. Come on, do it now while I'm with you.'

Moira pulled her phone reluctantly from her pocket and looked at Tessa.

'You can do it.'

Under Tessa's watchful gaze, she hit delete until his name was wiped from her phone. 'I don't feel any better.'

'You probably won't for a while yet, but you did the right thing.'

'Maybe.'

'Definitely.'

'So, I'll see you in just over a week?'

'You will.'

'Have a fantastic time, don't catch herpes off that old Blarney Stone and try not to think about what Big Jes got up to in Killarney when you reach the Ring of Kerry.'

Tessa laughed. 'I'm glad I've eaten, you'd have put me off breakfast reminding me of that.'

'Oh, and have a super, hot date with your man in Waterford.'

'I'm planning on it.' Tessa winked.

Moira got up then and gave her a squeeze. 'I'm glad I met you.'

'Me too.'

Chapter 29

'Jaysus what is she wearing?' Moira muttered as she came around the front of the red Ford Focus Mammy had replaced the Beemer with not long after Daddy passed. Aisling joined her sister giving their mammy the once over.

'They're fisherman pants, you know the sort people wear in Thailand on their hols. You don't normally team them with a black polo neck and boots though,' Aisling informed her sister. She'd not be holding her hand up to having once worn baggy elephant pants on a Bangkok stopover. 'All she needs now is one of those conical leaf hats and a scooter.'

Moira shook her head. The wide-legged pants might look the part in a tropical climate but on a freezing day beside the South Lough in the Powerscourt Estate's car park, they looked bizarre. 'I'd got only just gotten used to the nautical look.' Since she'd moved to the seaside village of Howth, Mammy had taken to wearing nautical striped tops, white pants, and boat shoes. Moira had never thought she'd say it but they'd at least looked the part.

'I can hear you,' Mammy said as the car bleeped and, satisfied it was locked, she stuffed the keys in her bag before joining her daughters.

The sisters were unabashed. 'Where did you get those pants, Mammy?' Aisling asked. 'They're very ethnic looking, so they are.' She eyed the green and gold swirls on the fabric dubiously.

'Shirley from golf gave them to me when she heard Rosemary and I had booked to fly to Vietnam. She got them on her holidays in Thailand last year.'

Aisling shot Moira an *I told you so look*, before saying, 'Do you not think you might have been better saving them for your trip to Vietnam?'

Mammy suddenly lunged, left leg forward. Moira was reminded of the Warrior pose she'd once done in a yoga class Andrea had dragged her along to. Her favourite pose had been Corpse. It had been great, lying there like she was dead, listening to swishing tides and seagull cries, very relaxing, her kind of exercise. Andrea hadn't wanted to go back though, she said yoga wasn't for her, she was after more of a cardio workout.

'What are you doing?' Aisling asked as they made their way toward the palatial entrance of the hotel.

'I'm showing you why I'm wearing them.'

'Right.' Aisling was bewildered but Moira just shook her head once more—and Mammy had the nerve to say *she* took things too far!

'See, I can do all sorts in them.' She squatted to prove her point.

'Mammy!' Moira hissed, fearful she might demonstrate the Downward Dog next, here in the regal grounds of the Powerscourt Estate. She cast around for CCTV cameras but couldn't spot any.

Mammy was not chastened, although she contented herself with taking giant strides instead of striking any more unusual poses. 'They're the comfiest pants I've ever owned, girls. Although I did manage to get myself into a bit of a tangle trying to do them back up after I'd been for a visit.'

'Jaysus, Mammy, that kind of visual could put a girl off her cakes.'

'Moira, I'd be quiet and quit while I was ahead if I were you or you won't be getting any cakes. You're still in my bad books.'

Moira did as she was told. She kept her mouth zipped all the way to the Sugar Loaf Lounge. The Georgian-styled lounge bar was busy. It was a popular destination with locals and tourists alike, and she was surprised Mammy had managed to secure them a table over by the windows. She relaxed into the mustard upholstered chairs and couldn't help but admire the glorious, albeit overcast view of the rolling Wicklow countryside. 'This is a lovely treat, Mammy, thanks.'

Maureen O'Mara looked appeased. 'So we'll not be having any more of you carrying on over me booking myself a nice holiday? Because I had a phone call from Roisin asking what I thought I was up to. She told me you put her up to it.'

Moira chewed her lip; her sisters were both tell-tale tits and she still had plenty to say about Mammy's trip but the fight had gone out of her today. She felt like a vacuum-packed bag that had had all the air sucked out of it. 'I shan't say another word.' Today at least she thought watching the staff scurrying back and forth with the three-tiered serving trays piled high with edible works of art. Mammy was chattering on about the plans she and Rosemary had been making for their trip with Aisling commenting in all the right places. She let their voices wash over her as her mind strayed to Michael. She wished she could get that intimate moment she'd seen him and his wife share in the entrance to The Saddleroom out of her head.

The arrival of their afternoon tea was a timely distraction from replaying the scene yet again. It seemed to get worse each time she ran through it. They'd be having a fecking grope in the entrance at this rate she thought, helping herself to a scone. It was deliciously light and fluffy and the dollop of strawberry jam along with the Chantilly and lemon curd that had had her taste buds in an anticipatory tizz earlier was divine. Except, today it wasn't. Today, it tasted dry, like cardboard, and the cream seemed to have a tang as though off. It wasn't the food, it was her because Mammy and Aisling were tucking in, pigs at a trough, making annoying little *mmm* noises, and *is yours good? because mine's lovely* remarks. She put the half-eaten scone back on the plate. It seemed Michael had broken her heart *and* killed her taste buds.

'What's up with you, Moira? It's not like you to let your sister get the rainbow coloured tiramisu cake.'

She looked over at Aisling who gave her a triumphant smirk. The said cake was on her plate and her fork was raised ready to do its worst. Mammy was right, it wasn't like her. Once she'd even rapped her sister hard over the knuckles with her teaspoon to prevent her from getting it. There was only ever one slice amongst the other delectable bites and if she didn't get it, things could get ugly. It was her favourite, and as such, she wasn't prepared to consider going halves.

'Nothing's wrong. I'm fine.'

Mammy put her fork down and swivelled in her chair to face her youngest daughter before pushing Moira's hair away from her face.

'What're you doing, Mammy, you've Chantilly cream all over your hands, you'll get it in my hair.'

Mammy stared hard at her through narrowed eyes. 'You've not been out doing the binge drinking again have you?'

'Jaysus, Mammy.'

'What? You drink too much, in my opinion, Moira. Every time I see you, you're green around the gills, so you are.'

'I'm not.'

'You are. I remember telling you the last time we went for lunch you looked like your Shrek woman, the Princess Fiona.'

Granted, that had been a particularly big night.

'I think it's man troubles, Mammy,' Aisling piped up, and at the word man, Maureen O'Mara's eyes lit up and she put down the shortbread she'd decided to nibble on next.

Moira glared at her sister and decided she'd pin the poster of Bono she'd had hidden on the shelf at the top of her wardrobe, waiting for the right moment, to Aisling's bedroom door when she got home. Her sister couldn't stand the Irish rocker, and a dose of Bono is what she'd get for landing her in it. It was a close-up shot of him too she thought, with a modicum of short-lived satisfaction, because Mammy was like a dog with a bone when it came to the man subject.

'Have you a man then, Moira?' The hope on her face made it shine and she looked almost angelic. Almost.

'No.'

'She does, or she did. His name's Michael.'

'Shut up, Ash.' Moira got her foot ready because if Aisling mentioned Michael's age, she was going to get a kick under the table.

Mammy looked at Moira questioningly.

'We had a fight,' she said limply. 'It's over.'

'A-ha! I knew it. He wasn't sick at all. You left your posh engagement party early because you'd had a barney.'

'Engagement?'

Moira almost laughed. Aisling had done it now. She'd said the 'e' word. Served her right. Her sister sat back in her chair sensing the error of her ways.

'Shirley from golf who gave me these pants, her daughter, she's younger than the both of you, by the way, is after getting engaged to a lovely young man. Shirley never stops talking about the wedding.' Mammy directed her attention to Aisling. 'How are things progressing with you and Quinn?'

'We're grand,' Aisling replied, feigning great interest in her cake.

Chapter 30

It was four o'clock by the time Mammy dropped Aisling and Moira back at O'Mara's. She pulled up outside the guesthouse and told them she couldn't come in. 'I've joined the yacht club and there're drinks being held in my honour at five. I need to get home and get changed.' Her foot was idling over the accelerator in readiness to take off.

Aisling opened the passenger door with, 'Are you expecting us to drop and roll, Mammy?'

Moira was guessing the nautical gear would be getting an airing once she got home. She clambered out the back and had barely got the door shut before she was gone. A flash of red disappearing down the road. Her head spun sometimes she thought, making her way to the door, with the volume of activities her mammy involved herself in. It was her way of filling the hole Daddy had left behind in her days, she guessed. She wished she could do the same, but she wasn't of a mind to take up golf or join a rambling group and she certainly wouldn't be seen dead in boat shoes. She heard her phone bleep the arrival of another message from somewhere in the depths of her bag and gritted her teeth. If it was from Michael, she didn't know if she'd be strong enough to ignore it this time around. She pushed open the door, Aisling close behind her and ventured inside.

Evie who came on at four was settling herself down behind the computer in the reception area while James, his shift finished, was slinging his backpack over his shoulder. Moira knew there'd be an empty lunch box and nothing else inside it. She marvelled over the amount of food the boyo could put away. Whenever she breezed past the front desk of a weekend, he'd be sitting there eating. Mrs Baicu, the mother of sons herself, had a soft spot for James and never failed to present him with a full Irish, more often than not he got a second helping, too. Bronagh had given him and him alone, permission to help himself to the custard creams and his mammy sent him off to work with a packed lunch fit for a king. She caught Evie eying him from under her lashes. He was a good kid, Moira thought. Give him another year and he'd be a proper heartbreaker.

James engaged Aisling with a brief run down on how his shift had gone. He'd only had one glitch when Mr Rochester in Room 5 came downstairs blustering about not being able to find his watch. James had located the Rolex down the side of the bed for him and everybody had been happy. 'Apart from that everything's been grand. I'll catch ya.' He gave a wave and pushed the door open ready to head home. For his tea, no doubt, thought Moira as Evie, a mournful look on her face as he shut the door behind him, took her headphones off.

The tinny sound of a Boyzone's hit *Everyday I Love You* rattled from her MP3 Player before she turned it off. She'd be deaf by the time she was thirty listening to it that loud, Moira frowned. It was a very odd, old sort of thing to have thought. She wasn't in her right frame of mind, she needed to get upstairs and check her phone in private. She also had a desperate urge to swap the dress she'd worn, knowing Mammy thought she looked well in it, for her pyjamas. She wanted to burrow in for the duration of the day and night.

Aisling moved beside the fax machine as it whirred into life, waiting to see what it would spit out. 'I'll check Ita's made up all the rooms on the list before I come up. We've a tour group arriving in the morning.'

'Hello, goodbye,' Moira said to Evie, who gave her a grin having forgotten about James—out of sight out of mind—young love could be fickle she thought, taking herself off up the stairs.

~

The message was from Andrea. Moira eyed it as she lay prone on the sofa with her striped pjs on. She didn't want to call her back. She'd done enough hashing through the events of the night before as it was. Her hand snaked inside the family pack of Snowballs and she popped one in her mouth. She'd discovered the half-eaten bag tucked away behind the tins of spaghetti. It was where Aisling always hid things she didn't want Moira getting hold of. Snowballs were Aisling's premenstrual go-to. She was adamant there were hormonal balancing ingredients to be found in the chocolate and coconut marshmallow balls. Moira didn't know about that, Aisling was always a snappy madam around that time of the month, but she was finding comfort in them.

She tossed her phone down next to her not knowing if she was disappointed or relieved that Michael hadn't tried to get in touch with her again. She was spared dwelling on it further by the front door opening and she leapt into action shoving the bag under the cushions in the nick of time. Aisling wouldn't be happy when she discovered her sister had been helping herself to her Snowball stash. There were times though when a girl had to do what a girl had to do to survive and right now Snowballs were hitting the spot—that was all there was to it.

Chapter 31

There was someone was knocking on the door, Moira realised, opening an eye. She'd been dreaming she was hammering on the bathroom door shouting at Aisling to hurry up, the way she did sometimes when she needed a wee. Her subconscious mind's way of waking her up. The knocking sounded again. Whoever was there was determined she thought, trying to rouse herself and wishing Aisling were here to answer it but knowing she'd be downstairs. The tour group from America was arriving this morning; she'd have her hands full settling them in. Feck it, she murmured out loud tossing the covers aside. She clambered out of bed and slid her feet into her slippers, which for once were easily located beside the bed. Her eyes were bleary as she made her way to the door, sure it was Andrea on the other side. That girl got up far too early on a Sunday morning. No doubt she was annoyed because she hadn't returned her call last night.

She better have bought croissants with her Moira thought, flinging the door open and blinking stupidly. Surely, she was still dreaming? She closed her eyes firmly this time and counted to three before opening them again. He was still there. It wasn't a holy vision backlit by the landing lighting but Michael. He was dressed in the casual weekend clothes she'd only glimpsed him in a couple of times and he was only just visible behind the enormous bunch of red roses he was holding out to her. She looked at the spikey, delicate blooms, registering at the same

time that she must look like a wild woman in her Marks &
Spencer's flannelette pyjamas. Moira took the term bedhead to
a different level most mornings and she instinctively raised her
hand to smooth her hair.

'What are you doing here?' Jaysus, she was such a mess.

'You haven't returned my calls. I needed to know you were
okay.'

'I'm fine apart from being caught out in my pyjamas.' She
wasn't fine, far from it, but for once the lie tripped easily from
her tongue.

His smile was wan. 'You probably don't want to hear me
say you look beautiful right now, but you do and I uh, I
brought you these.' He was still holding the roses out to her she
realised and, against her better judgment, she took them from
him without comment.

'Can we talk?'

She was glad Andrea was not here. Had she been lurking in
the vicinity she would have snorted and told her the man was a
walking cliché and to tell him to sling his hook.

'I don't think there's anything to say, Michael.'

'Please, Moira. Let me explain.'

She should shove the roses back at him, call him a fecker,
and shut the door in his face but she hesitated and that was all
he needed.

'Five minutes, Moira, please, that's all I ask. Five minutes to
explain and then I'll go if you want me to.'

It was the earnestness in those twin, ocean-coloured pools
that swayed her. She stepped aside allowing him past, 'It's
through to the left,' she said as he hesitated and followed him
into the living room. Aisling had drawn the curtains and she

caught a glimpse of an uncommonly clear sky. It was going to be one of those bonus winter days where the sun shone and you could almost fool yourself into thinking spring had arrived early. She went into the kitchen and placed the flowers down on the bench unsure as yet what she'd do with them. Put them in water? Or perhaps they'd be better in the bin in the courtyard downstairs away from her sister's twitching nose. She wouldn't want Foxy Loxy scratching his nose when he poked inside it, though.

Michael took in his surrounds, his anxiousness made visible by restless hands. 'This is a great space,' he said, for want of something to say, and Moira nodded before gesturing him over to the sofa. She had no intention of joining him, she'd be staying right where she was thank you very much with the kitchen bench top serving as a barrier. He removed the empty pack of Snowballs peeking out from behind the cushion, looking at them bemusedly before putting it on the coffee table. He perched on the edge of the sofa, not quite at home, not yet. Good, Moira thought, staying right where she was. She could smell the coffee Aisling had made for herself this morning and she felt a pang for caffeine but it would have to wait, she wasn't going to let Michael stay any longer than the time it took for him to say his piece.

'I had no idea you were going to be at the party,' he offered up, seeing she was waiting for him to get on with it.

'Clearly. I wanted to surprise you and I obviously did.'

'Adelaide only came because Noel Price would frown on a spouse not attending. He's old school, but he's also my boss, Moira, and I have to play the game.' He massaged his temples.

Adelaide. Moira realised it was the first time she'd heard him say his wife's name.

'God, what an awful night. All I wanted to do when you left was run after you and make sure you were alright.'

'Like Prince Charming.'

He looked a little mystified. 'I've never had that comparison made before, but yes, I guess so, like Prince Charming.'

'Only Cinderella had made a holy show of herself and you stayed right where you were by your wife's side.' The word 'wife' resounded like a verbal slap.

'I wanted to go to you, Moira, believe me, I wanted to but I couldn't show Adelaide up like that. It wouldn't have been fair.'

'Ignoring me the way you did wasn't fair.' Her voice climbed an octave and she didn't like the note of hysteria in it. 'And I saw the way you looked at each other.'

He looked at her beseechingly. 'You saw a couple who've known each a long time, Moira. That's what you saw. We're good friends, I told you that, but that's where our relationship, apart from a piece of paper that says we are married, ends.'

She wanted to believe him, she really did. She also bloody well, really wanted that cup of coffee and she turned her back on him to give herself a moment to think. 'Do you want a tea or a coffee?' She flicked the kettle switch.

'I'd love a coffee.'

She knew how he liked it. White with one. They'd sat nursing a cup of coffee each only a week ago, talking about how they'd both like to visit New Orleans one day. Moira wanted to go there because her daddy had loved the Dixieland jazz—she'd grown up to the sounds of his Louis Armstrong records. It would be a homage to visit the Big Easy as he'd called the river city. It had floated unsaid between them that perhaps they might stroll the French Quarter together. The café's smell of warm baking and cinnamon that afternoon had permeated the part of her brain where she stored the things she wanted to hold on to. Those moments she could pull out and relive when the lid on the painful compartment wouldn't lock properly. She set about making the drinks, banging and clattering the cups and the teaspoons to fill the silence.

'Thank you,' he said, as she handed him his cup his eyes searching hers. 'My car's parked outside. There's somewhere I want to take you, if you'll let me.'

Chapter 32

'Thanks for agreeing to come, Moira.' Michael held the passenger door of his silver car, with its sporty undertones, open and she clambered into the bucket-style black leather seat, glad she'd had the foresight to wear jeans. This car was not skirt friendly unless you wanted to share your smalls with all and sundry who happened to be walking down the road. Nor was it a car for family outings she thought, feeling comforted by the fact, even if her arse did feel as though it were inches away from scraping the tarmac. She pulled the seatbelt across her chest buckling in as he got behind the wheel. He opened the glove box and produced a tape.

'Do you like Moby?'

Moira nodded and while he messed around with the CD player, she glanced back at O'Mara's. It had been a relief to make it out the door without bumping into Aisling. She was grateful too that James was more interested in dipping his soldiers into the yolk of his fried egg to care who she was going out and about with. It would have been a different story had gossipy little Evie been manning the fort.

Michael gunned the engine as the familiar beat of *Why Does my Heart feel...* reverberated around the interior. The traffic was light and he zipped his way through the city streets. Moira leaned her head back against the seat, content to let the music wash over her. It was only when the housing began to disperse giving way to wide open spaces that she finally spoke up. 'So then, are you going to tell me where we're going?'

'We're nearly there, you'll see.'

~

Moira stared at the plane they were walking toward across an expanse of green field purporting to be a runway in disbelief. 'You're not planning on taking me up in that are you? It's tiny. It looks like something my nephew, Noah, would play with.'

'That there, is the Cessna 172. She's a four-seater work-horse. One of the safest planes ever built.' Michael waved over to the handful of people milling about inside the hangar to their left. There were two other similarly small aircraft housed inside it and they were faffing around the planes the way a man going through his mid-life crisis might his new Ferrari. Boys and their toys Moira thought, beginning to drag her heels. She could feel her boots sinking into the winter-soft ground, but Michael was having none of it. He reached out behind him for her hand and pulled her along. She liked the feel of hers co-cooned protectively inside his. She could do this.

'You said it yourself, you've only ever flown Ryan Air. You'll love it. Although I can't promise any in-flight service.'

'Neither can Ryan Air,' Moira muttered, and he laughed.

'Touché. Afterward, if you fancy it, I thought we could go and check out Lough Tay, it's supposed to be nice right?'

He seemed confident all was forgiven; indeed Moira could feel herself unpicking the knot of doubt as to what he'd told her about his other life with every step they took. 'The Guinness Lake, yes it's gorgeous.'

'Does it really look like a pint of the black stuff, as you say?'

She nodded, picturing the lake viewed from the hilltop. Its black waters were deep and mysterious and with the white sands of the beach on the northern side it really did look like a pint of Guinness.

'A good spot for a picnic?'

She nodded. It would be busy. It was always busy there because it was on the tourist trail but there was safety in numbers. She wasn't ready to take the next step with Michael, not yet.

'Good, because I'll have you know I slaved over the rolls and cakes I packed.'

'Did you?'

'No I stopped at Tesco's, I thought it best to leave the picnic preparation to their bakery department experts.'

She laughed, the confusion and upset of yesterday was beginning to dissipate like slowly dissolving bubbles in a bath—almost a forgotten memory.

He really was pulling out all the stops, but what had she let herself in for Moira wondered a second later as she hoisted herself into the passenger side of the plane. She eyed the panel of knobs and dials with mistrust as Michael settled in behind the controls. 'Relax, Moira, the conditions are perfect. I wouldn't take you up otherwise.'

'Have you taken Adelaide flying before?' She hadn't expected to ask that question and it felt strange acknowledging his wife out loud to him by saying her name, but his answer suddenly mattered very much to her.

'No, she doesn't like heights. She won't fly unless it is an absolute necessity.'

Moira's shoulders relaxed and she let him help her on with her headset and microphone, pushing her hair away from her ears. His touch sent an electric shiver through her and she was certain her pupils had just dilated to twice their normal size. Michael didn't appear to notice, he was intent with getting on with the job at hand. 'You won't be able to hear me otherwise,' he said, checking she was belted in before doing the same himself.

She gritted her teeth as the plane rumbled into life and the propeller spun around. It began to bump down the grassy runway and she closed her eyes. If she'd had her rosary beads with her, she would have begun reciting Hail Marys. Instead, she contented herself with clutching the seat, knowing without looking her knuckles were white. The last time she'd felt like this was when she'd had her wisdom teeth out and at least then there'd been gas.

'Here we go!'

Moira peeked at Michael in time to catch the slightly mad gleam in his eyes. It was the look of someone who thrived on speed, on danger, she thought clenching her buttocks for good measure too, as the plane picked up speed. She squeezed her eyes shut again not enjoying the sensation of the ground slipping away beneath them as the plane juddered into the air.

'You can open them now,' Michael said, his voice sounding tinny in her ear.

She did so and squealed. The sky was the road ahead and she peered out her window and watched in wonder as the fields became a patchwork quilt, each segment a different shade of green, the livestock on the ground mere specks. It took her a beat to realise the fear of the unknown had shifted and given way to a new sensation. She was aware of a surge coursing through her and realised it must be adrenalin. It swiftly liquified to fear as the plane buffeted up and down. She was sitting in a tin can with a propeller stuck to the front of it and the sudden jerking served to remind her that can was no more than a tiny blip in a vast sky.

She side-eyed Michael to see if she could pick up on any panic on his face but he was completely chilled, obviously enjoying himself. He must have sensed her eyes on him. 'It's fine, Moira. You feel the turbulence more in a smaller plane than you would in a larger one. They're just air pockets.' Her nerves began to untangle themselves as the seconds passed and they didn't begin a sudden nose dive toward the ground like a seagull honing in on a fish. She grew used to the plane's movement and as the time ticked by was aware of a big grin she couldn't have wiped from her face even if she'd wanted to. So, this was what it felt like to be a bird she thought as Dublin stretched out beneath her like toy town. She, Moira Lisa O'Mara, was flying.

~

'What did you think?' Michael asked as they made their way back to his car. The time had passed swiftly and Moira had no idea how long they'd been in the air.

She felt like yelling, 'I'm alive!' but it brought Frankenstein to mind so instead she said, 'It was incredible, thank you.' She wanted him to hold her hand like he had before.

'It's addictive.' He flashed her a grin, and if there'd been any angst or doubt left inside her where he was concerned, it melted like the last of the snow in spring.

'I can see why.'

She felt like they'd shared an intensely personal experience. Something that no one else could understand. A bit like when you had really fabulous sex, she mused. It had been just them up there in that big blue sky, alone in the world. She could see why people did crazy things now. Why they threw themselves out of planes with nothing but a modified sheet to keep them from hurtling to the ground, or why they leapt off the side of tall buildings with a piece of elastic tied to their ankle. That sensation of the blood rushing through your veins as your heart pumps wildly—it was thrilling because you knew in that moment you were alive, properly alive. Not that she had any plans to sky dive or bungee jump! No, this morning's adventure had been enough living on the edge for her. Or had it?

Michael held his hand out to help her step over the crater-sized puddle beside the gate to the car park entrance. She'd only narrowly avoided it on the way in and she took his hand, holding on tightly for fear he'd let her go once she'd jumped over it. A Land Rover that hadn't been there earlier was parked next to his car but nobody was in it. There was a van too, but again it was empty. The car park was deserted. It was just the two of them and Moira decided it was her turn to take charge. She tugged at his arm to stop.

'What's up?'

'Nothing.' She didn't want to think, she just wanted to act and she snaked her free hand around the waist of his jeans sliding her fingers inside the belt loop in order to pull him in to her.

He opened his mouth to speak, but she silenced him, standing on tiptoes and covering his mouth with her own. She kissed him with the intensity of someone who'd thought her heart had been broken only to find it miraculously mended. He groaned and she felt his arousal. She didn't want to go picnicking she wanted to go somewhere where they could be together, properly together.

'Do you know somewhere we could go?' She didn't have to explain herself, he understood her meaning.

'Are you sure?'

'I'm sure.'

Chapter 33

Michael navigated the winding lanes back to the main road deftly, with one hand on the steering wheel. Moira's hand rested on top of his as he changed the gears. Neither spoke, and the air in the car hung heavy with anticipation of what was to come. The silence was only broken by the bleep of a text message arriving. It was Michael's, but he didn't pull over to check his phone. He was in a hurry to get where it was they were going and the realisation sent a thrilling tremor through her.

Where would they go? Moira wondered as the green belt gave way to suburban houses. Where was it people who had to be discreet went, a hotel? She supposed so. It hadn't mattered when they'd met for drinks or dinner. Those outings could be easily explained away but visiting a hotel in the middle of the afternoon was another matter altogether. Dublin was a small city on a world scale, three degrees of separation and all that. The odds were if they were to check in somewhere edgy and cool like The Clarence, U2's hotel, they'd see half of Mason Price on a Sunday team-building excursion at the pub across the road or something like. She didn't fancy a seedy alternative down a back alley much either. They didn't head toward the city though; they were moving in the direction of the airport and for a fleeting moment she allowed herself a fantasy whereby they flew to Paris and lost themselves in the city of love.

Michael was indicating she realised, hearing the steady tick-tick-ticking as he waited to turn in. She looked past him and saw, not the Eiffel Tower but the perfectly respectable looking Crowne Plaza Airport hotel. A transient place where people went when they needed to put their heads down between flights. It was ideal. There would be no knowing looks from an Evie type on reception because it was reasonable to assume they'd flown in from somewhere far away and couldn't face the long drive back to their little village down south. She was getting carried away with her different scenarios she realised, putting it down to a cocktail of nerves and excitement.

'Will this be alright?' He looked concerned that she approved. 'I mean it's not where I'd choose to take you had I time to arrange things but—'

She silenced him by leaning over to kiss him. 'It's fine. Next time you can take me to Paris.' She smiled to let him know she was joking.

'I would love to take you to Paris.'

His phone began to ring as they got out of the car. He retrieved it from his pocket and looked at the screen. She wondered whether he would ignore it again but he flashed her an apologetic smile, 'I won't be long, you go ahead and wait for me in reception.'

She walked toward the entrance trying not to think about who might be on the other end but the sound of his voice carrying toward her on the snappy afternoon breeze stopped her.

'Is she going to be alright? The words burst from him like a gun being rapidly fired. 'What happened?'

Moira turned around and saw his ashen face, hearing him say, 'I'm on my way.' He disconnected the call and shoved his phone in his pocket as Moira ran back to him

'What is it? What's happened?'

He was already moving to unlock his car. 'Ruby's been knocked down by a car. She's being taken to St James's, now.'

'My God, is she alright?'

'I don't know, Adie, said she's unconscious; that's all she knows. I'm going to meet them at the hospital.'

'Here, give me your keys. You've had a terrible shock, I'll drive you.' She held out her hand, but he didn't toss her his keys. Moira felt something shift and change between them in that split second of hesitation before he climbed behind the wheel. Of course, he didn't want her driving him, he couldn't have her dropping him off at the hospital. How could he explain that while his and Adelaide's daughter had lain in the road broken and possibly dying, he'd been caught up in his own lusty emotions with her? She heard him say he was sorry before he slammed the car door shut and gunned the engine, leaving her standing in the hotel's forecourt.

~

Moira paid her fare and sat down in an empty seat near the back of the bus. She stared out the window at the grey high-rises of Ballymun, seeing but not seeing as the bus rumbled back toward the city. She hadn't stopped praying for Ruby to be alright since Michael had driven off. She didn't think she could live with herself if she wasn't. As the bus lurched to a stop to pick up more passengers, she chewed her bottom lip in contemplation of everything that had happened since those fateful boardroom drinks when she'd first seen Michael.

Had she read too much into their relationship if it could even be called that? Had she built him up to be more than he was in her mind because she'd been trying to fill the gaping hole in her life? She'd thought the times they'd spent together, although snatched, were special, but she was wrong. The realisation sat heavily on her shoulders. What he had with his family was special. Just like the relationship she'd had with her Daddy had been special. Who was she to muscle in on his family? And yes, she knew it wasn't all down to her, but had she chosen to hear and believe what she wanted? It was all tainted now, the more she thought about him the more what they'd had become skewed like the image in a funfair mirror.

It seemed to take an age but, at last, she pushed the bell and clambered off the bus. She'd call in to Tesco's and pick up a couple of bottles of red. She very much wanted to drown her sorrows.

Chapter 34

Moira clinked in the door of O'Mara's and Evie looked up from her phone. Curiosity was stamped to the young girl's forehead as she called out a hello. It was swiftly followed by, 'Have you got company coming tonight, then?' She eyed Moira's shopping bag. The temptation to tell her to mind her own business was great but she couldn't be dealing with Aisling wanting to know why she'd gone and upset their young receptionist, even if she did agree she was a nosy madam.

'Just stocking up, Evie.' Her tone made it clear she wasn't up for a chat and she took to the stairs, hoping as she made her way to the third floor that Aisling wouldn't be home and she could be left with her Tesco's specials, three for the price of two Chilean reds in peace.

The apartment was empty and Moira put the bottles of wine down on the kitchen bench before moving to switch the television on. The silence, only broken by the monotonous ticking of the grandfather clock, would make her feel like she was going mad. She wanted some mindless background noise. She also wanted to get out of her jeans and into her pyjamas which seemed to be getting a good innings of late. She went to get changed, sitting down on the edge of her bed to check her phone in case she'd somehow managed to miss an incoming message from Michael. She was desperate to hear how Ruby was doing but the screen was blank.

Her pjs were where she'd stepped out of them that morning. She'd felt so buoyant and hopeful of things working out after all as she'd thrown her clothes on while Michael waited for her in the living room. How could things change so fast? she thought, pulling the bottoms on before buttoning the warm flannelette top. She paused as she made to leave the room to look in the dressing-table mirror. She half expected to see someone she didn't know staring out at her because she felt different, numb yet raw. All her nerve-endings were flayed and exposed. The wine would help calm her she thought, amazed to see the face in the mirror was pale but apart from that exactly the same as it had been that morning.

~

The silence from Michael was deafening Moira thought, knocking back her fourth or was it fifth glass of wine. She was onto the second bottle she knew that much. She'd left three messages asking him to call her, concentrating on not slurring the words together as she'd asked how Ruby was. The room had taken on a softer glow, the familiar shapes of the furniture blurring so she was uncertain whether there were two armchairs or one, one grandfather clock or two. She was still on edge, but the panicked thoughts as to the state the teenager might be in had grown muted, and fuzzy around the edges like the furniture, with each mouthful of the claret liquid.

Moira pulled herself up from the sofa and wobbled her way over to the bench—she'd just have one more glass.

Chapter 35

'Moira Lisa O'Mara, this is your mammy speaking, wake up.'

A nightmare? Moira thought she was having a nightmare whereby Mammy was about to rip open her curtains and tell her she was sleeping her life away, the way she'd done when she was a teenager. She opened one eye seeking verification it was all a bad dream and squeezed it shut again as the light sliced through her retina and pierced the part of her brain that had shrunk to the size of a dehydrated pea. Her tongue, she realised, was stuck to the roof of her mouth. She didn't want to wake up fully and suffer the hangover she knew was lying in wait, preparing to smother her the moment she acknowledged she was compos mentis.

'Moira, I will drag you out of that bed if you—'

She opened her eyes and groaned. It wasn't a dream, it was horribly real. Mammy's face was inches from hers and as she inhaled, she wondered if she was about to be put out of her misery with an overdose of Arpège perfume. 'I'm awake, please go away.'

'Good, that's a start and I'm not going anywhere. There's a cup of coffee and two Panadol on the cabinet here for you. Now do as you're told and sit up.'

Moira was too weak to argue and she dragged herself up to a sitting position. She leaned her head against the wall. She really did feel like she was dying and she had no idea what she'd done to deserve to be woken by her mammy when she felt this terrible. She reached over for the coffee, her hand shaking as she picked up the mug. She heard Mammy tut something about the 'state of yer' before she scooped up the Panadol and holding them out to her, told Moira to swallow them down with her drink.

She did so and slowly the coffee penetrated the fog in her head as she pieced together what had happened yesterday with sickening clarity. Had Michael phoned? She knew she'd left messages on his phone asking him to but she'd have slept through a freight train crashing through her bedroom given the state she must have been in. She cast around frantically for her phone. It was on the pillow next to her and she snatched it up to see if there were any missed calls or messages to check. There was nothing and she tossed the phone back down in frustration. She would ring the hospital herself she resolved. She'd say she was a relative, so they didn't block her with their silly privacy laws.

She couldn't remember going to bed and assumed she'd staggered off of her own accord when the wine ran out. Her eyes flitted to her bedside clock and she nearly dropped the mug. 'Mam, it's after ten! I should have been at work an hour and a half ago.'

Mammy paused, the pile of clothes she'd picked up off the floor in her arms. 'Calm down and finish your drink. The coffee will sort you out so it will. Your sister had the foresight to call in sick for you when she couldn't wake you up.'

So she had Aisling to thank for Mammy being here to administer her unique brand of TLC. Her face must have given her thoughts away because Mammy said, 'And don't you be giving out to Aisling about telling tales. She phoned me because she's worried about you. I don't blame her either. I don't blame her at all. I mean just look at you, Moira, look at the state of yer, and you a grown woman not a teenager who doesn't know when to stop.' There was no muttering this time. Her message came across loud and clear.

Moira didn't say a word as she drained the cup and hoped she didn't bring the strong black liquid back up again. It swilled uncertainly in her tummy for a moment but then decided to stay where it was. Mammy finished putting the clothes away in the drawers and took the mug from her. 'Right-oh, my girl, in the shower.' She shook her head. 'I could get drunk just off the smell of yer, and those sheets are for the wash. You're a disgrace, so yer are.'

Moira wasn't looking forward to being upright but she could tell by Mammy's face she wasn't messing. There was nothing for it, she'd have to get up. She threw the covers aside and stood up. The room spun around her and it took a few seconds for her to feel steady enough to make her way to the bathroom. The sheets were already being ripped from the bed before she reached the door. She didn't hang around and once safely inside the bathroom she wet a flannel and held it to her face.

A glimpse in the mirror as she dropped the flannel into the basin a minute later revealed a horror show of roadmap eyes and dry chapped lips, and she grimaced before brushing her teeth. She turned on the shower, looking forward to letting the hot water wash over her sore head and, leaving her pyjamas in a heap, she stepped under the jets. It did help ease the throbbing behind her eyes and as she shampooed her hair, she wished she could wash away the events of yesterday as easily as she could the soapy suds. How was Ruby? she wondered for the hundredth time, reaching for the bodywash. By the time she stepped out of the shower she knew she smelled a lot sweeter than when she'd stepped into it. She could have stood under the spray until the hot water ran out but didn't want to further incur the wrath of Mammy.

Spying her smelly old pyjamas she turned her nose up; she didn't want to put them back on and so, wrapped in a towel, she made her way to her bedroom. It was like a fridge she thought, shivering and seeing her bed had been stripped. The sheets were undoubtedly spinning around in the machine right at this moment. The curtains billowed out startling her, no wonder it was freezing, Mammy had yanked the window up to let some fresh air in.

She took her time getting dressed despite the chill air because she didn't want to face the music and she knew, without having to look, Mammy would be in the living room tapping her foot impatiently. She'd be sitting in Aisling's favourite chair over by the big windows like a judge presiding over her courtroom waiting for the accused to be brought before her. Moira had been there before, not for a good long while but it was all coming back to her including the feeling of trepidation knowing she was in trouble.

She checked her phone again and this time her heart leaped as she saw she'd had a call. It sank immediately as she was it was from Andrea. Her message said it was urgent and for her to call her back on her mobile as soon as she could. She held the phone in her hand for a moment, should she call her back? She probably just wanted to find out if Moira was bunking because of what had happened at the party on Friday night, too embarrassed to front up. She hit speed-dial before she could change her mind and stood by the window, huddling inside her over-sized sweater, waiting for Andrea to answer.

'Where are you?' she demanded after three rings.

'I'm at home and I *am* sick; self-inflicted but believe me I'm sick.'

'Moira, you know Sunday sessions are the work of the devil come Monday morning,' Andrea chastised.

'Don't go on at me. Mammy's here and she's on my case.'

'Oh dear, you're in big trouble then.'

'I sure am.'

'Have you heard about Michael?'

'What about him?' The drama in Andrea's voice made her stomach clench and her innards threatened to liquefy as she sent up a silent plea for the news not to be bad.

'His youngest daughter's after being in an accident. He's not in work either and the news has being going around the office like Chinese Whispers all morning.'

'I know she was hit by a car and I'll explain how I know in a minute, but please, Andrea, just tell me is Ruby going to be okay?'

Andrea must have picked up on the desperation in her voice because she didn't argue. 'She will be. She fractured her leg and her pelvis and I did hear something about internal bleeding but she didn't have any head injury which was the big worry, apparently. She was lucky. It was her fault so everyone's saying. She didn't look just stepped out on the road and the poor man driving the car had no show of stopping. At least he wasn't speeding.'

Moira didn't know if a fractured pelvis and leg could be called lucky but she was alive and she was going to be okay. That was the main thing. She collapsed on to the bed needing to feel something solid underneath her as the news soaked in.

'Are you still there, Moira?'

'Yes. It's a relief that's all. I was with Michael when it happened.' Andrea listened in silence as she filled her in on the events of yesterday finishing when she reached the part where Mammy had woken her up.

'At least you didn't sleep with him, Moira, and what happened to his daughter is not down to you. Don't you start blaming yourself. Her accident is not some form of karmic retribution.'

'I know that, I do, but I can't stop thinking about how while she was lying there on the road injured, I was thinking about having sex with her dad.'

She heard a sound in the doorway and her heart flew into her mouth, she'd done it now. 'Andrea, I've got to go.'

'I think you and me need to have a chat about what exactly you've been up to, Moira O'Mara.' Mammy said.

Chapter 36

Moira didn't know where it came from but as she sat statue-still on the bed, the phone warm in her hand, something bubbled its way up inside her. It erupted into a sob and once it had escaped the floodgates opened and a torrent followed. She dropped the phone and held her head in her hands as her body racked with violent unstoppable shudders. She felt herself getting pulled in to an Arpège embrace but this time she gulped in the scent desperate to cling on to her mammy. The hole she'd been skirting around since her daddy died had just widened into a chasm and she was teetering on the edge terrified if she fell in, she'd never be able to clamber back out.

'I'm scared, Mammy.'

'Shush, now. I'm here. Whatever it is we can fix it.'

'Mammy, what's going on?' Aisling's voice sounded from the doorway. 'Moira, what's happened?'

Moira felt her sister sit down on the other side of her and her arms wrap around her so she was cocooned between her mammy and her sister.

She choked out the words she'd been holding inside, 'I miss Daddy.'

'Ah, sweetheart I do too. He was one in a million your daddy. I miss him all the time. It's like an ache that won't go away.' Mammy's voice was choked.

'That's how I feel too,' Aisling sniffled, joining in.

They stayed like that for an age until Moira's crying began to abate to small kitten-like hiccups.

'Come on,' Mammy said. 'I'll make us all a nice cup of tea. Aisling, go downstairs and ask Bronagh for a packet of her custard creams, tell her it's an emergency.'

~

Moira was sprawled on the sofa, the blanket Mammy had tucked around her threatening to slide off as she leaned over and dunked her biscuit. She quickly popped it in her mouth before it could collapse into her tea. She instantly felt better for the sugar hit. She'd held nothing back, she'd told Mammy and Aisling all about Michael and was grateful that, for once, they'd just sat and listened. They didn't pass judgment until she'd reached the bitter end. Then, there'd been some debate whether the relationship could even be deemed a relationship given it hadn't been consummated—Mammy's word—it had made both Aisling and Moira cringe. It was decided that it didn't matter if any riding—Aisling's word—it had made Mammy blanch, had taken place or not. The intimacy of the conversations, the feelings they'd shared, the kisses, they all amounted to an affair, of the heart at least, and if they were Adelaide—what kind of name was that?—they'd see it as a betrayal—both their words. The main thing was, Mammy said, fixing Moira a no-nonsense gaze, was that it was all over and done with now.

It was, Moira had told her. She meant it too. This time there'd be no going back. She'd seen it in Michael's eyes when he'd taken Adelaide's call. It had dawned on him in those awful seconds he could lose his family. She didn't want to be responsible for that. She'd mend. People didn't die of a broken heart, or at least she didn't think so. Ruby would heal too. It would just take time that was all.

Aisling had cocked her head and sighed. 'I'm going to check on Ita. I asked her to hoover the second-floor landing but I can't hear anything. The last time I saw her she was sitting on the stairs on her phone. I don't know what we pay her for, I really don't.'

'Ah, sure don't be giving out. I've known her mammy for years, she's like an aunt to you so she is. Ita's a good girl, Aisling, she just needs a prod here and there.'

'Foot up the arse, more like.'

'What was that?'

'Nothing.' Aisling rolled her eyes in Moira's direction before heading off in search of their Director of Housekeeping, leaving her sister to the remainder of the biscuits. Mammy was transferring the wet sheets into the dryer.

'I think going to see someone you can have a chat to about how you've been feeling might be a good idea, Moira.'

'What do you mean, see someone?' Her hand hovered over the last two biscuits as she visualised lying on a sofa. Much like she was now come to think of it, only in a darkened room with a wizened old man with huge glasses on, writing notes on a pad as he asked her how she felt. No, not a good idea she concluded.

'A grief counsellor. I should have suggested it after yer daddy passed but it was all I could do to get out of bed each morning. I went and had a few sessions with a lovely lady. I think it helped, a little anyway. But hitting the bottle the way you've been isn't the answer,r Moira.'

'Did you have to lie on a sofa?'

'No, I sat in a chair.'

'Did she wear big owl glasses?'

'No.'

'I'll think about it then.'

'Now then,' Mammy said, setting the dryer to run and heading in Moira's direction. 'Scrunch up, I've something else to tell you.' She sat down next to her with her hands clasped in her lap as she told Moira that Rosemary had cancelled her trip to Vietnam.

'Are her hips not up to it?' Moira feigned sympathy. It would seem she could scratch her plans to employ good cop, bad cop tactics with Aisling where this holiday was concerned.

Mammy gave her a funny look. 'Nothing to do with her hips and all to do with the new fella in our rambling group she's got her eye on. She's frightened if she goes away Breda Mc-Grath will get her hooks into him. It's a blessing in disguise, Moira because I've had an epiphany this morning.'

Moira could feel her headache returning as Mammy picked up her hand and held it in hers, giving it a squeeze for good measure. 'I still think grief counselling is worth a go but a change of scenery after well, all this other Michael business will do you the world of good. We'll make it a mother-daughter, trip. You and me against the world, kiddo.'

Moira cringed at her faux-American accent but it went over the top of her head.

'A break from hitting the sauce won't do you any harm and then when we get home, we can reassess your drinking see if we need to look at getting you some professional help.'

'But Mammy—' This was a waking nightmare.

'But Mammy nothing. We'll have a grand time, so we will.'

Chapter 37

Tessa hefted her bag on to the wooden luggage rack at the foot of the bed. She was back in Room 1 of O'Mara's and arriving here this afternoon had felt like coming home. Bronagh on reception had greeted her like a long-lost friend and Aisling had appeared from the guests' lounge with a cushion in her hands to ask her how her road trip had been. She'd chatted with the two women until the phone had begun to shrill and she decided she'd better let them get back to their work. Before she let Aisling return to her cushion plumping though, she asked her if she'd mind booking a table for three at Quinn's for seven that evening. Aisling had beamed—it was business for her boyfriend after all—and said she'd be delighted to.

Tessa opened her case and eyed the neatly packed contents. Was it worth unpacking for the sake of a night? No it wasn't, she decided. Instead, she pulled out her coral dress and shook it out. She'd worn it to dinner with Owen and he'd told her she looked stunning. The memory of the lovely evening they'd shared made her smile. She'd really liked him and hoped they would keep in touch because, you never knew what could happen. The world had suddenly opened up with possibilities for Tessa and she marvelled over how much more enjoyment there was to be found in life once you stopped letting negative thoughts and feelings weigh you down.

Next, she retrieved her toilet bag which she put in the bathroom and then she dug down in the bottom of the case for her travel clock. The time was just after four she saw opening it and setting it down on the bedside table. Moira wouldn't be home until at least six and she'd surprise her with the dinner reservation she'd made then. She hoped she and Andrea could make it, otherwise she'd be dining alone and she desperately wanted an update on all that had happened in the time she'd been away. A yawn escaped her lips. It had been a busy day. She'd been on the road early in order to get the car back to the hire place at the agreed time. There'd been a lot of faffing around when she got there over the mileage but it was sorted in the end. She deserved a little afternoon siesta she decided, lying down on the bed and enjoying stretching out on the soft covering.

~

'This was a grand idea, Tessa,' Andrea said, still smiling over Alasdair's ebullient greeting of them as she sat down. They had a table near the window tonight and could either watch rugged-up Dubliners getting from A to B under the glow of the street lights or turn their attention to the fireplace and be mesmerised by the dancing flames in the fire. Paula, their waitress, passed the menus out and informed them that today's special was a hearty slow-cooked Irish stew. It was the sort of meal that would warm you right through after being bitten by the cold evening air and Tessa remarked that's what she planned on ordering.

Moira had been anxious about bumping into Tom, not that she could tell Tessa and Andrea this. She also knew she couldn't avoid Quinn's forever and now they were here and he was nowhere to be seen she felt a little let down.

'Wine?' Tessa asked. 'This was my idea and it's my farewell dinner treat so order what you like.'

'No, be fair, you paid last time. Andrea and I are getting this, and I'm off the sauce but don't let that stop you two having a drop.'

Tessa raised an eyebrow. 'I can see I've some catching up to do.'

They sorted the drinks, a homemade lemonade for Moira and the house red they'd enjoyed the last time they'd been here for Tessa and Andrea. It didn't take them long to make up their minds as to what they wanted for dinner and once they were all comfortable, Moira took a deep breath and launched into her tale. Andrea was abreast of all the goings on and she sipped her red quietly while Moira filled Tessa in on what had happened in her absence. She interrupted when Moira told her how she'd dreaded going back to work with the likelihood of bumping into Michael.

'Awkward,' Tessa murmured.

'Yes. He's politely reserved when I do see him, and if he can avoid passing by reception he will, which I'll admit stings a little, well a lot. Feelings aren't taps. You can't switch them on and off, but it is the way it has to be. I get that and I accept it, it's just hard that's all.' She stirred the ice in her drink around with her straw. 'On the bright side, the egg sandwich food poisoning story seems to have been taken at face value. Mairead told me she's sticking with cheese sarnies from now on.'

Tessa laughed and then her face grew serious, 'Your mother's right, you know. A break away will do you good. It will help you get some perspective.'

'Yes, but I could get some perspective on a sun lounger in Spain, not backpacking around Vietnam with my mammy.' Moira shuddered, she still couldn't believe that in a week's time she was going to be winging her way to Asia. The thought of sitting on a plane, London to Ho Chi Minh, for fourteen odd hours with Mammy, well, she didn't know what she'd done to deserve it. Actually, that wasn't true—she knew exactly what she'd done to deserve it. She hadn't even been able to play the *I can't get time off, Mammy* card. Work when she broached it with HR, had been surprisingly understanding about the sudden request for time off and she'd start showing Amanda, the South African temp, the ropes tomorrow.

'Ah, sure it's quality bonding time for the pair of you.' Andrea's snigger didn't escape Moira and she poked her tongue out at her before turning to Tessa.

'So that's me, how was your holiday, or more to the point, how was dinner with yer man Owen?'

They ordered their meals while Tessa told them about Owen. 'Typical isn't it? I finally find a man I'd like to take things further with than a first date and he lives on the other side of the world.'

'How did you leave things?'

'We agreed we'd like to keep in touch and who knows?' She shrugged. 'He might pay me a visit in Auckland. He said he's always wanted to visit New Zealand and now he's got the perfect excuse to. Failing that, I'd love to come back to Ireland again at some point in the future. I thought I'd moved on, that my life was in Auckland, but I've loved being back; it's home too, you know?'

The two women nodded although they couldn't imagine living anywhere else than Dublin.

'What about you, Andrea? Is there anyone you've got your eye on?' Tessa asked, realising she knew the ups and downs of Moira's love life but had no clue as to Andrea's.

'I've had my eye on Connor Reid at work forever but he's got his eyes on an Amazonian accountant. Unrequited love is a bugger.' It was said lightly but Moira knew her friend found it tough. She saw him every day of the week; she hankered after him and spent her lunch breaks reading things into nothing where he was concerned. He never looked her way and, in her opinion, it was time Andrea moved on in her affections too but that was easier said than done. She knew that first-hand.

'You need to cast your net wider,' she told her friend. 'Give somebody else a chance, sure there're loads of fellas who'd love to take you out.'

'Who?' Andrea demanded.

'Well, there's yer man in IT, Jeremy wotsit.'

'He doesn't fancy me.'

'He does so, he always makes fixing your computer a priority.'

Tessa smiled listening to them banter back and forth.

By the time their mains arrived, steaming piles of deliciousness, the topic of conversation had moved on to long-haul flights.

Moira was listening as Tessa recommended using a mineral water spray to stop your skin drying out and not to drink alcohol.

'Fat chance of that anyway,' Moira muttered. 'I've promised Mammy I won't touch a drop between now and when we get home from our trip. I suppose I was knocking it back any opportunity I got. It had become a bit of a bad habit and it won't do my liver any harm to have a breather. I must say it's been nice waking up in good form too.' She'd had to explain to Mammy that yes, she was prone to drinking too much, but she wasn't an alcoholic. She could stop, it was just she hadn't wanted to because she liked the fuzzy, numb feeling she got when the hard knocks life had delivered after her daddy's passing got to be too much. It was a fine line she was walking, Mammy had said with her finger wagging and so Moira had decided to prove to her that she didn't need to drink. It was her choice whether she did or she didn't. To be fair, she was finding it strange not having her customary glass of something or other bolstering her, but she'd get there. Habits were hard to break.

She was about to fork up a mouthful of the cottage pie she'd opted for when she saw Tom. He was crossing the restaurant and making for the kitchen. Her heart began to race. He hadn't seen her so, what should she do? Ignore him and hope he didn't notice her on his way out? Or brazen it out and go over and say hi. Without the red wine egging her on she was shy and embarrassed but she still felt she owed him an apology.

She wiped her mouth with the napkin and pushed her seat back before she could change her mind. 'Excuse me a moment, I've just seen someone I need to say hello to.' She could feel Andrea and Tessa's eyes on her back as she called out to Tom before he pushed the door open into the kitchen and disappeared.

'Moira.' He grinned seeing her. 'How're ya doing?'

'Oh, I'm grand enough. Listen I wanted to apologise again for, you know,' she knew her face was strawberry pink.

Tom looked surprised. 'Ah, sure you're grand; forget about it. So, how is he? The eejit you were seeking revenge on by using my body?'

Moira's mouth curled upwards. 'We called it quits before it even began really. I'm going off on a bit of a compulsory adventure for a while with my mammy to Vietnam. We leave next week.' She realised she sounded like a child off on her hols with her mammy. 'It's a long story as to why I'm going with my mammy. I didn't have much say in it, and to be honest I hope we don't murder each other. We'll be joined at the hip for nearly a month.'

He laughed. 'I'd love to hear that long story some time. Vietnam, though, wow! I spent six months backpacking around Asia. Thailand, Vietnam, Laos, and Cambodia, it was fantastic.'

They grinned rather inanely at one another.

'Well...' Her cottage pie would be getting cold but for some reason, she wasn't in a hurry to get back to it. He had kind eyes and she liked the way they were appraising her. 'It was nice seeing you, Tom. I'll get back to my dinner then.'

'I only called in to pick up my pay; it was a bonus bumping into you again.'

Moira hesitated but wasn't sure what to say or do.

'I'd love to hear all about your trip when you get back. You know relive my backpacking glory days vicariously. Maybe we could go for a meal? Not here, obviously, somewhere where I can sit and eat, too.' His eyes twinkled invitingly as he added, 'Now that the eejit is history.'

Moira looked at his expectant handsome features. She needed to work on herself before she went out with anyone else. Would it be fair to say yes only to realise she wasn't ready, she wasn't over Michael? She'd be leading him on a second time. Then again, he'd made her smile and there was that cute bum of his to take into consideration. Oh, for goodness' sake, Moira, she admonished, he's not asking you to marry him, it's only dinner. 'I'd like that, Tom, thanks.' They grinned stupidly at one another once more before Moira turned and walked back to the table. She knew the big silly grin was still plastered to her face but she couldn't help it.

She realised as she sat down and Andrea and Tessa chimed, 'Well, what was all that about?' that the fugue she hadn't known she'd been walking around in since her daddy passed had lifted a little. Through the grey fog there was a pocket of bright blue. The future, once she got this ridiculous trip with Mammy out the way, might just hold rainbows and sunshine after all.

The End...Almost

The red fox set about his familiar night-time routine. He padded stealthily over to the gap he'd dug under the bricks that separated the park that was his home and the courtyard beyond. He poked his nose through the hole and sniffed the air. It was damp and filled with all the usual scents of chimney smoke and late suppers that would make a poor winter-starved fox's nose twitch. It was silent at this time of the night unlike the daytime when the gardens he lived in were filled with life and he burrowed down deep to sleep. This courtyard that was home to his favourite bin was a dangerous place in the daylight hours and he stayed away knowing the round, red-faced woman who meant him harm with that rolling pin she wielded lay in wait.

For now though, he was safe and he eased his bristly body through the cavity, his ears pinned back as he listened out. The only sounds were far away from him and his beloved garbage bin. He began his pitter-patter march toward it. The scraps had been sorely lacking of late; it had been an age since he'd tasted the sweet creaminess of white pudding or the savoury tang of its black cousin but he never lost hope that the bin would yield a feast. A sudden noise, the sound of a window squeaking open made him freeze and his yellow eyes darted upwards to its source.

She was there again, the girl who used to toss him treats until one day she'd stopped. She was bigger now her face sharper than it had been but her hair still hung long, the colour of the night. Her face was ghostly in the light from her room as she smiled down. 'Hello again, you. I've brought you something.' She shook what was wrapped in a napkin out and it landed with a soft thud by his front paws. His heart soared, his luck had turned, it was a large sliver of his beloved white pudding!

He snatched it up, and marched with his tail held high back to his hole in the wall. As he squeezed through, he heard her call down, 'I'll see you tomorrow night, Foxy Loxy.' These humans were a funny lot he thought, melding into the darkness on the other side of the wall.

Hi! I hope you enjoyed Rosi's Regrets and that the story made you smile, or even better laugh out loud. If you did then leaving a short review on Amazon to say so would be wonderful and so appreciated. You can keep up to date with news regarding by books via my newsletter (I promise not to bombard you!) and as a thank you receive an exclusive character profile of the O'Mara women: www.michellevernalbooks.com[1]

What Goes on Tour

Book 3 – The Guesthouse on the Green Series

Moira and Maureen O'Mara aren't on your usual mother, daughter trip. You won't spot them browsing the shops on Grafton Street followed by a spot of a lunch in Dublin's iconic Bewleys. Oh no, Moira and her mammy have just arrived in Vietnam.

It's Maureen's dream to sail on a Junk (who knew?) and as for Moira, well she's come along for the ride under duress—Mammy made her. Join them as they travel the hop on-hop off bus from Hoi Chi Min to Hanoi.

Along the way Mammy and Moira get to know Sally-Ann. She's an Australian who has very different reasons for being in Vietnam. She and her late husband served there during the war and his dying wish has brought her back to a country she vowed she'd never return to.

By the time the bus pulls into Hanoi's Giap Bat bus station, Sally-Ann learns you don't need blood ties to be family and Moira and Mammy will see each other through different eyes.

Join Mammy and Moira O'Mara on their journey of self-discovery.

---

1.   http://www.michellevernalbooks.com

Printed in Great Britain
by Amazon